T0123438

THE PATRIARCH

PREVIOUS BOOKS BY ALAN REFKIN

FICTION

Matt Moretti and Han Li Series

The Archivist
The Abductions
The Payback

Mauro Bruno Detective Series

The Scion
The Artifact

NONFICTION

The Wild Wild East: Lessons for Success in Business in Contemporary Capitalist China
Alan Refkin and Daniel Borgia, PhD

Doing the China Tango: How to Dance around Common Pitfalls in Chinese Business Relationships
Alan Refkin and Scott Cray

Conducting Business in the Land of the Dragon: What Every Businessperson Needs to Know about China
Alan Refkin and Scott Cray

Piercing the Great Wall of Corporate China: How to Perform Forensic Due Diligence on Chinese Companies
Alan Refkin and David Dodge

THE PATRIARCH

ALAN REFKIN

 iUniverse®

THE PATRIARCH

iUniverse books may be ordered through booksellers or by contacting:

iUniverse
1663 Liberty Drive
Bloomington, IN 47403
www.iuniverse.com
1-800-Authors (1-800-288-4677)

ISBN: 978-1-5320-9835-2 (sc)
ISBN: 978-1-5320-9836-9 (e)

Library of Congress Control Number: 2020905791

Print information available on the last page.

iUniverse rev. date: 04/08/2020

To my wife, Kerry
To Anna and Calogero Bruno

PROLOGUE

The thousand residents of the Italian town of Mezzegra, on the northwestern shore of Lake Como, forty miles north of Milan, realized that their location was both a blessing and a curse. Located on arguably the most beautiful lake on the planet, Mezzegra attracted hordes of tourists who congested the streets and made it nearly impossible to find a table in a restaurant. The blessing was that tourists provided the bulk of employment in an area that was substantively devoid of other economic opportunities.

The southern end of the town was dominated by Saint Benedict's Monastery, which sat at the top of a hill and had a commanding view of the lake. Erected in 529, it was a complex of four fortress-like buildings of undressed stone, with flat buttresses at the corners that were used to reinforce the structures. The walls of each building were thick, and the windows were kept small to prevent the five-story structures from collapsing upon themselves. Once home to over two hundred monks who produced magnificent illustrated manuscripts, it now housed two dozen who focused on prayer, community service, and giving tours to anyone who paid the twenty-dollar entry fee.

The interior of all four buildings was spartan and unremarkable except for the library, which housed more than thirty thousand manuscripts and bound books, some of which dated as far back as the sixth century. The four-thousand-square-foot room, with cocoa-brown tile flooring, oak desks and shelves, and a vaulted wooden ceiling, had received Band-Aid-type repairs for centuries until finally succumbing to neglect a decade ago and collapsing upon itself. It likely would have remained a pile of broken wooden beams and scattered stone had it not been for an American philanthropist who had once toured the monastery. Learning of its plight, he financed a five-year reconstruction, restoring the library to the grandeur it had displayed a millennium and a half ago.

Once the construction was complete, the librarian had the unenviable task of moving the multitude of manuscripts and books, which had been stored hastily throughout the monastery, to the newly installed shelves and drawers. He refused all help from the other monks because they weren't familiar with the library's numbering system. One mistake, he told them, and whatever was misfiled would likely be lost forever. While he was placing books on the shelves, he came upon two large leather volumes that were without title. Curious, he carefully unfastened the metal buckles that bound their weathered black leather flaps and found that each book had been hollowed out to hide a raft of papers.

It immediately caught his attention that the top of each page was embossed with a colored imprint of two crossed keys, one gold and one silver, bound together with a red cord—the seal of the papacy. Looking closely at the pages, he saw that they were in fact vellum, parchment made from the skin of a calf. Each page was the same size, seven inches wide and nine and a half inches long. The writing on the vellum was in purple-black iron gall ink, which had faded little in the nearly three centuries since the date atop the first page.

As he placed the two stacks next to each other on a table, he noticed that one was half an inch taller than the other. Curious, he glanced at the first sheet in each stack. Both pages were written in Latin, a language he'd studied since his days as a novitiate, and they appeared to be duplicate Vatican financial ledgers from the early eighteenth century. But upon closer examination, he realized that the monetary values for the same entry in each ledger were significantly different. Moreover, the thicker ledger included entries that weren't listed in the other. He put his finger on one such notation, dated October 1, 1735. The thicker ledger listed a donation of 10,500 scudi from a patron. But only 105 scudi was recorded in the thinner ledger. Looking through more pages, he concluded that the thicker ledger was probably accurate, since it recorded numerous sales of Vatican assets that weren't listed in the other.

As the monk looked through the two stacks of vellum pages, the discrepancies continued. The most interesting page, however, was not in either ledger—it was a piece of vellum that had been placed at the bottom of the thicker stack. This page bore the embossed crest of the Vatican's secretary of state at the top, which the librarian was able to identify thanks to a Google search, and a red wax seal featuring the same crest at the bottom. In the center of the page were the words "Archivum Arcis Armarium D 217," and below that was the signature of Cardinal Ettore Casaroli. The librarian didn't have the vaguest idea what these Latin words referred to, since the translation into Italian was "the archive cupboard area." He wondered why these words were so important that a pope's secretary of state had signed his name and affixed his wax seal below them. Obviously, he had wanted someone to know he was the author of these words. But why? And what was the archive cupboard area? He'd heard of the Vatican archives, sometimes referred to as the Vatican Secret Archives. Was this what the cardinal was referring to? After decades of boredom in his position of handing out books and returning them to shelves, he decided to play detective and find out.

CHAPTER 1

S ALVATORE BRUNO WAS the chief prosecutor for the city of Milan. The eighty-two-year-old widower was five feet six in height, weighed 140 pounds soaking wet, and had thinning gray hair that showed a small bald spot atop his head. He walked, despite his advanced age, with a posture that was nearly ramrod straight, and he had perfect twenty-twenty vision thanks to cataract surgery that also had corrected his nearsightedness. He'd worked as a city attorney for four decades, occupying his current position for the last three. During this time, he had married and had two sons, one of whom had died at an early age. The other was a chief inspector with the Polizia di Stato in Venice. He was unabashedly proud of his son, who was widely acknowledged by the state police as the most formidable investigator in Italy.

The chief prosecutor had grown up Catholic, which some viewed as almost a requisite for Italian citizenship. He went to church every Sunday, on Holy Days of Obligation, and sometimes in between if, as he told those he worked with, he needed guidance from a higher authority on a case. Although Venice and Milan were only 175 miles apart, he saw his son only two to three times per year—usually on his birthday, Christmas, and possibly the anniversary of his wife's death.

This wasn't because both men didn't deeply care for one another. On the contrary, each was the other's best friend. It was because both understood that they were married to their jobs. Their governmental wives were extremely demanding, requiring their attention twenty-four seven. Thankfully, Salvatore Bruno's late wife had understood their marriage wasn't monogamous. Mauro's late wife also had accepted this work ethic because she was a police officer and therefore understood the demands of the job.

It was a seminal day for the chief prosecutor following his visit from the mayor. During that meeting the mayor had handed Salvatore two volumes of centuries-old documents, each protected on the top and bottom by weathered black leather flaps that were fastened together with a metal buckle. They had been given to the mayor by a former classmate and longtime friend, the abbot of Saint Benedict's Monastery. The circumstances of how the abbot had come upon them weren't provided, but they showed possible wrongdoing by the Rizzo family, the head of whom was traditionally referred to throughout Italy as "the patriarch" because of his immense financial and political power. The current head of that family was Duke Rodolfo Rizzo.

Salvatore Bruno and Rizzo hated each other with a passion. It was well known that the chief prosecutor had long been looking for anything that would give him the hard evidence required to prosecute the person he believed was behind the majority of local and government corruption and smuggling and a laundry list of other offenses, including murder. Three decades as Milan's chief prosecutor had given Bruno a mountain of circumstantial evidence against the patriarch, enough to put an ordinary person away for life. But since Rizzo had more attorneys and judges on retainer than the prosecutor's office had employees, Bruno was seldom able to even interrogate him. Nearly every time he tried, one of Rizzo's attorneys would get a judge to issue a court order preventing the interrogation. Often that would be followed by an admonishment from the court. And on the rare occasion when Bruno decided to file a criminal complaint and forgo interrogating the patriarch, that was always followed by a judge dismissing the case before it even went to trial. Most Italians believed that the patriarch was a criminal in a pinstripe suit but didn't care because his actions had no effect on their daily lives. Therefore, in the best Italian tradition, it was che sarà, sarà—whatever will be, will be.

After the mayor left, Bruno told his deputy, who had been in the office when the mayor handed him the two volumes of documents, that the reason they were being given these papers was that they involved the Rizzo family. The situation was therefore a double-edged sword—which in politics was one edge too many. He remarked to his deputy that if these documents implicated the patriarch's family in criminal activity, and the investigation led to a guilty verdict, then the mayor would take full credit for what had occurred, which was standard practice for every mayor Bruno had worked for. On the other hand, if Bruno accused the patriarch's family of a crime and failed to obtain a conviction, then the mayor would turn on him in a heartbeat—also standard practice for every mayor he'd worked for when expectations didn't conform to reality.

Bruno put both volumes into his black Floto Firenze briefcase for safekeeping, locked it, and left for the day carrying the elegant leather bag tightly in his right hand.

Once the chief prosecutor was gone, his deputy went into his office and closed the door behind him. He then removed a burner phone from his jacket pocket and phoned his second and better-paying employer.

Duke Rodolfo Rizzo had an expression of annoyance on his face. The reason for this contortion of facial muscles was the deputy prosecutor, who'd inadvertently called the patriarch's cell and interrupted his aperitif at the Four Seasons La Veranda restaurant. Normally, Rizzo would have answered the call without reaction, even if he had a $500 A5 Kobe steak in front of him. But when one was about to imbibe in a Hennessy Beauté du Siécle Grand Champagne cognac, the dynamics changed. Every busboy, server, and sommelier at the restaurant understood this and left him alone to pour the delicate golden liquid from the ornate bottle that he'd brought with him into his snifter. They understood that he wanted to take his time and savor the rare cognac by first wafting its sophisticated aroma, then looking at its elegant color, and finally activating the right combination of taste buds as its complex sapidity passed over his palate. Therefore, when the staff at the restaurant heard his cell phone chime, they adopted the same sour expression that Rizzo displayed. In the early stages of his ritual, and undoubtedly not wanting to rush his enjoyment, the patriarch answered the call.

Moving to a smaller table in the corner, which offered better privacy, Rizzo listened to the deputy chief prosecutor relate his meeting with the mayor and describe the two stacks of vellum pages, which he referred to as ledgers, that had been given to Salvatore Bruno for safekeeping. The patriarch's expression didn't reveal surprise at what he'd been told, even though he couldn't answer how a copy of these ledgers existed outside his family diaries and papers, which were in a two-story vault in his study. He concluded that since both volumes had come from the abbot of a monastery and were dated from the time of Cardinal Ettore Casaroli, the abbot probably had somehow come into possession of a second set of books from the first patriarch's partner.

From his placid facial expression, an observer would assume that what the deputy chief prosecutor had said didn't faze Rizzo in the least. Any crimes documented in the ledgers had occurred nearly three centuries ago and didn't involve him, and a PR firm could spin this and blame any number of people from three hundred years ago, real or imaginative, although the cardinal would be the easiest target. As Rizzo was about to end the call, the deputy chief prosecutor said that he had one additional bit of information. In addition to the ledgers, the mayor also had handed Bruno a single piece of vellum. It carried the wax seal and signature of Cardinal Casaroli. Above, the cardinal had written the words "Archivum Arcis Armarium D 217."

When the patriarch heard this, he dropped the Baccarat snifter holding his precious cognac onto the brick patio, shattering it into a dozen pieces and bathing the bricks below him with roughly $5,000 of the golden liquid. His look was not placid now. Instead, he looked as if he'd been told that he was sitting on a pressure-sensitive bomb that would detonate the moment he stood.

CHAPTER 2

LUCIANO GISMONDI DIDN'T look like an assassin. At five feet four and 130 pounds, the diminutive thirty-five-year-old killer, with short black hair and a neatly trimmed beard, did not seem a threat. All his life, he'd gone unnoticed, and today was no exception. Dressed in a black cassock and a four-winged Biretta hat, he strolled past the guards outside Milan's city hall in the Piazza della Scala and past security at the opera house across the street without receiving so much as a second glance. As he walked, he exuded what some might consider an air of arrogance—a ramrod-straight posture, an unsmiling face, and the avoidance of eye contact with those around him. But his perceived demeanor had less to do with attitude and more to do with the fact that he had a McMillan TAC-338 sniper rifle with folding bipod under his religious garment and taped to his back.

His target was the mayor, who had a well-known daily routine of walking from his office to the nearby Park Hyatt Hotel for lunch. It was a stupid hole in his security, but one that Gismondi was thankful existed. Even so, what he was about to do wouldn't be easy. The mayor would be a moving target, and Gismondi's bullet would take almost two seconds to reach him, dropping thirty feet along its trajectory. There was no question he could make the shot; ten years as a sniper in the Italian Special Forces Target Acquisition and Reconnaissance Regiment had given him the necessary skills to kill at even greater distances. Even so, he had told his employer that he would have preferred to wait and shoot the mayor in a less public setting. But the patriarch wasn't known for his patience or for tolerating failure. His verbal employment agreement could be summarized in three sentences: Success was rewarded with wealth, women, expensive toys, and anything else one might desire. Failure resulted in all these pleasures being taken away. Abject or multiple failures had only one outcome—death. During the five years Gismondi had worked for Duke Rodolfo Rizzo, there had been two other assassins. They were all kept busy because the patriarch didn't resolve his disputes in a court of law; he disentangled himself from them by eliminating the problem. Not long ago, Gismondi had been ordered to kill one of his counterparts when their employer decided that his lack of performance could no longer be tolerated. The jury was still out on the other assassin.

Entering the apartment building he'd reconnoitered earlier that day, he took the stairs to the fifth floor and knocked on the first door to his left. If no one came to the door, he'd pick the lock. If someone did, well ... Unfortunately, an elderly man answered the door with a look of irritation on his face that said he wanted to know who the person was in front of him and why he was being intruded upon. This look was soon replaced by a vacant stare when Gismondi, in one smooth motion, took the knife that he'd been hiding behind his back and thrust it into the left side of the man's skull. Dragging the body into the apartment, Gismondi kicked the door shut. He put on a pair of latex gloves and searched the apartment to ensure that no one else was inside.

With less than an hour before his target would leave for lunch, he took off his cassock, removed the disassembled rifle that he'd taped to his back, and began reassembling his firearm. Once that was done, he dragged the kitchen table across the room so that it rested against the wall, just below the windowsill. Unfolding his bipod, he lay prone on the table as he looked through the scope of his rifle and canvassed the area around him. Seeing nothing unusual, he focused on two flags, one halfway to his target and the other behind it, for telltale signs of changes in wind. At this distance, with the longer flight time and slowing of the bullet's velocity, even a small change in wind direction or intensity could result in his missing his target.

Thirty minutes later, right on schedule, two security guards escorted the mayor out the revolving door of city hall. The guards walked on either side of their charge as the trio proceeded down the long flight of steps leading to the street. Opening the window just wide enough to expose the tip of his rifle barrel, Gismondi aimed his crosshairs at the center of the mayor's torso. It didn't matter where precisely the .338 Lapua Magnum round impacted, even though he was a thousand feet away. The mayor's death probably wouldn't be caused by the bullet itself, but by the energy its shock wave imparted on the body's organs. The resulting cavitation would destroy these critical body parts and bring about an almost instantaneous death.

When the mayor was halfway down the stairs, the assassin exhaled briefly, then continued to let out his breath as he slowly applied 2.5 pounds of trigger pressure. The rifle's retort was loud, and when the two security guards beside the mayor heard the shot, they instinctively grabbed him and fell to the ground. But they were too late; they were lying atop a dead man.

Leaving the untraceable weapon and bipod on the table, Gismondi donned his cassock and hat, left the apartment, and placed his latex gloves in his pocket. He needed to hurry because there were two monks at a nearby monastery who needed to get to the pearly gates much earlier than they were planning, and he had a narrow window in which to start them on that journey.

The patriarch's hired assassin looked innocuous in his monk's attire as he left the monastery. It was his favorite disguise because religious men were almost always assumed to be harmless. Earlier today, he'd phoned the abbot and asked for a 4:00 p.m. meeting, requesting that the librarian also be present. He had indicated that he was calling on behalf of their American benefactor and that the philanthropist was interested in funding other renovative needs at the monastery. The abbot had readily agreed. Gismondi had scheduled the meeting for the period when the monks would be cloistered in their rooms for their requisite two-hour time of prayer and reflection, a fact he had obtained from the monastery's website, along with the name of their American benefactor. He had asked his employer about interrogating both men, but the patriarch said his informant had told him that within the monastery, only the abbot and the librarian knew of the ledgers. Therefore, interrogation would be an unnecessary risk and waste of time. Accordingly, when Gismondi arrived at the abbot's office, there was no discussion, only a surprised look on both men's faces when they saw a monk standing before them, holding a silenced Glock. Gismondi killed each man with a double tap to the head before they could comprehend what was happening.

Now there were only two men left on his kill list, and he'd take care of both tonight. He'd begin with Chief Prosecutor Salvatore Bruno, who he had been told had the ledgers in a large black briefcase that he always carried with him.

Gismondi had originally planned to break into Bruno's home, kill him, and retrieve the two thick stacks of vellum pages. But the patriarch wanted the chief prosecutor's murder to look like an accident because he had discovered through a Google search that Bruno's son was a famous detective in Venice who was widely respected for his highly tuned investigative skills. Therefore, after giving the matter some thought, Gismondi had devised a plan to kill the chief prosecutor by placing him on the losing end of a car accident. Luring Bruno to a place where that accident could happen involved killing the two monks first and then waiting for the chief prosecutor to travel to the site of the murders—standard procedure for the prosecutor's office in a homicide since the scene was within the jurisdiction of the Milan prosecutor's office. To ensure that Bruno and not his deputy would be the person to go, Gismondi had had the patriarch tell his informant to feign an illness.

The next phase in orchestrating Bruno's accident was, in the view of both Gismondi and the patriarch, the weakest link in the chain because it would involve bribing two yet unknown truck drivers to crash their rigs at a predetermined place and time. Although Gismondi initially had no idea who these truckers would be, he expected to find them at a rest stop near Mezzegra and gain their cooperation by offering them a substantial amount of cash. As it turned out, the assumption that he would be able to do so was correct.

It was late at night as Salvatore Bruno's tired red Fiat Panda grudgingly wove its way along the winding mountain road. Three sides of the emphysemic vehicle were enveloped in black as it trudged down the narrow strip of loose dirt circumventing Mezzegra, with its weak headlights making it difficult to navigate the road's numerous twists and turns. Although Bruno couldn't see more than fifty feet in front of him, he was familiar with this alternate way into Milan. He'd navigated this road, off and on, for sixty of the eighty-two years he'd lived in the area. He would have preferred to take the main highway, but a collision between two trucks had closed it. Consequently, he had been forced, along with any other local who knew of this route, to drive on what amounted to a dirt path if he wanted to get to Milan before the wrecks were cleared—whenever that would be. Another option would have been to return to the monastery, where he had been called to investigate a double murder, and use one of its spartan rooms. But Saint Benedict's was thirty minutes behind him. Another possibility would have been spending the night in one of the small towns nearby. But the prosecutor's meager office budget didn't have enough fat in it to pay the exorbitant rates the inns in these towns charged at this time of year. Therefore, with neither other option seeming especially appealing, and being familiar with the road, Bruno had decided to take the mountain pass road to Milan in his feeble and nearly blind car.

The dirt path from Mezzegra to Milan had been used since the time of Julius Caesar, and possibly before that, to travel from the Lake Como area to Milan. In modern times, locals used it as an alternate route to Milan when there was a maintenance or traffic issue on the main highway, which was not an uncommon occurrence. But most avoided taking it at night because there had been several fatalities over the years when drivers had missed one of its unforgiving hairpin turns. Focusing on the road, which had no guardrails, lights, or reflective strips, Bruno kept his car well away from the edge and the three-hundred-foot drop to the rocks below.

As the aging Fiat stubbornly navigated the path, a set of headlights approached from the rear. The fact that there were two people crazy enough to drive this path at night was unusual, but the fact that one was tailgating the other could be considered close to insanity. Bruno watched as the taillights eventually closed the gap between them and the car hit his bumper. When that happened, he instinctively slammed on the brakes to try to bring his car to a halt, so that he could speak with the driver before both vehicles had a catastrophic accident. But the powerful machine behind him maintained contact with his bumper and, even worse, began to accelerate. The Fiat's tires were smooth from age, so it had virtually no ability to stop given the force that was pushing it from behind. It began to slide on the loose dirt as it approached the hairpin turn.

Turning the steering wheel counterclockwise as hard as he could, so that that his car would turn into the mountain and away from the borderless edge of the path, Bruno waited for his vehicle to respond. When it did, the car that had been pushing it immediately disengaged. Unfortunately, by that time the Fiat had built up enough momentum that holding a foot on the brake wasn't going to stop the car before it reached the edge of the road. What was needed was a radical change in direction, and even though that command had already gone from the steering wheel to the two front wheels, the Fiat's response was sluggish because of the smooth tires and soft dirt. It failed to make the hairpin turn and flew off the edge of the road. Bruno held the steering wheel tightly in his hands, maintaining his grip until the vehicle tilted nearly ninety degrees downward. With the sudden pitch forward, he was no longer able to hold on and flew into the windshield, shattering it and rendering himself unconscious as he plummeted into the abyss below.

Gismondi had stopped his car and was looking through his night-vision goggles as the action unfolded before him. Pulling forward to the edge of the path, he got out of the vehicle and looked at the carnage below him. The Fiat had left a trail of debris clinging to the brush and the hard dirt outcroppings on the lower part of the mountain where it had impacted, before rolling down the remainder of the mountain to the riverbed. Not far from the flattened and demolished vehicle, the assassin saw Salvatore Bruno's motionless body. Since the briefcase he was looking for could be in the debris field below him or close to the vehicle, Gismondi decided that his time was better spent going back to Milan and killing the deputy chief prosecutor, the last person on his kill list, and then returning at first light to search for Bruno's briefcase, which he probably had no chance of finding in the dark.

CHAPTER 3

Jerusalem, AD 326

EMPRESS HELENA AUGUSTA sat in her throne-like wooden chair and watched as the last remaining slabs of stone from what had once been the Temple of Venus were dragged down the muddy hill. Her son, Emperor Constantine the Great, supported the excavation and had given his mother unlimited access to the imperial treasury, in addition to lending her part of his army to dismantle the largest temple of the time and probe beneath it. The structure she'd ordered demolished had been designed by Emperor Hadrian nearly two centuries ago and had, according to her research, something so valuable hidden beneath it that a description of what was encapsulated there had never been officially consigned to paper. Since the precise location of what she was looking for wasn't given, she had decided to demolish the entire temple.

Today the workers were at the only unexcavated portion of the site, and excitement was running high as soldiers stood shoulder to shoulder and plunged their shovels into the ground, expecting to find what they'd been looking for shortly. Each of the men performing the backbreaking daily routine of demolition and excavation had been told that something of great importance was beneath them and that once it was found, they would be generously rewarded. Since this duty kept them out of war and well fed, and they had an opportunity to attain wealth, the soldiers assigned to the empress were vigilant and worked without complaint.

For more than a week, the men toiled at this singular spot, removing bucket after bucket of dirt and stone until one man's shovel struck what appeared to be a large cistern, which was too deep to be part of the temple they'd dismantled. Word of this discovery spread, and soon Helena Augusta was standing over the group of shirtless men as they began to clear the surrounding area. With the soldiers working carefully throughout the night and into the following day to avoid damaging the four-hundred-square-foot waterproof enclosure, the cistern was gradually revealed. All were surprised and looked in confusion at it, apparently wondering if this was what they'd been searching for.

At that moment the one person who could answer that question was walking in their direction. Heads bowed as the empress approached. She ordered that the cistern be opened and patiently waited while the heavy rectangular watertight cover was removed, after which she stepped into the enclosure. The interior was dry, and no air had been able to enter, which meant that the contents were likely to be well preserved. Taking the torch that was handed to her, she found a *titulus*, a sign bearing a condemned person's name, inches from her foot. Bending down to take a closer look, she realized that it probably had become detached from the object beside it, which was quite possibly what she'd been searching for. She told the person who had handed her the torch that she required another test to irrefutably prove the authenticity of what had been discovered and ordered him to go to the residence where she was staying and bring back the person she'd brought with her from Rome. That woman would be the final authority to authenticate the object in question.

It took an hour for the woman to get to the excavation site, during which time the empress remained in the cistern and continued to study not only the object next to the titulus but also the other objects she had discovered there. Finally, a woman of advanced age was helped to the site of the discovery and down into the cistern. She now stood next to the empress. In a moment the authentication process would be complete.

Rome, February 1740

Pope Clement XII slowly made his way to his bedroom with the help of two Swiss Guards, each holding one of the eighty-eight-year-old pontiff's elbows, trying to take as much weight off his feet as possible. The five feet four bishop of Rome, whose aristocratic face bore an aquiline nose, thin transparent skin, neck-length gray hair, and intelligent eyes, refused all offers to carry him. His gout, which had returned two weeks ago, had swollen and inflamed his ankle joints to the point that each step was agony. Nevertheless, even though he needed assistance in walking to his quarters, what he was conveying to the curia, the ensemble of Vatican departments that advised him, was that he wasn't on his deathbed and was therefore still in control of church policies and decisions. Some within the apostolic state thought he should abdicate the papacy since he was not only frail but also completely blind. But Clement continually squashed all such speculation, saying that his service to the Holy See would end with his last breath, which those attending him knew only too well was a short time away.

Clement had ascended to the papacy at a time when there were so many opposing factions within the College of Cardinals that no member of the conclave was close to receiving the two-thirds majority of votes necessary to become leader of the church. Back then, he was looked upon as a relic who was unlikely to live much longer, given that his age was more than twice the life expectancy of the day. Because of this, he was largely ignored as a candidate for pope by those sealed within the Sistine Chapel. That viewpoint changed when the leaders of the various warring factions in the curia acknowledged that they were hopelessly deadlocked and required more time than the conclave would give them to negotiate among themselves and find a cardinal who would be acceptable enough to receive the necessary votes. This group, which controlled over two-thirds of the votes, decided that they would elect a placeholder as pope—someone who would govern the church as more or less a caretaker and not make any significant decisions. Most importantly, this placeholder must be likely to die within a year or two.

Cardinal Ettore Casaroli, a robust man in his late sixties with thinning gray hair, five feet eight in height and weighing over three hundred pounds, came up with the candidate. As the secretary of state for the recently deceased Pope Benedict XIII and the leader of one of the warring factions in the curia, he immediately thought of Cardinal Lorenzo Corsini from Florence. The seventy-eight-year-old, who was almost two heads shorter than Casaroli, had been largely forgotten by those in the curia because no one had deemed him important enough to include in their discussions. That changed once Casaroli mentioned his name.

On July 12, 1730, Cardinal Lorenzo Corsini became Pope Clement XII. As someone unfamiliar with the administration of the papacy, the newly elected pope asked Casaroli to remain as secretary of state, a position within the church that many referred to as the "deputy pope," since the secretary of state was charged with running the day-to-day affairs of the Vatican. Clement knew that Casaroli had powerful friends and political deftness, but he viewed both of these factors as strengths.

For nearly a decade, Pope Clement readily accepted his secretary of state's advice, allowing him to run the administrative and financial affairs of the Vatican. The periodic reports he received from Cardinal Casaroli indicated that the Vatican's financial stability, though not necessarily good, continued to show steady improvement. The pope was told that this improvement came at a price, however, because the needed operating capital was derived from the sale of Vatican land and art. But as Casaroli explained, there was no other way to eradicate the massive debt that had been incurred by the previous pontiff's excessive spending and corruption.

Over the years, as Clement's secretary of state extolled the improving financial situation, holes began to appear in his story. Clement had overheard rumors among his staff of graft and venality within the curia, the inability of the church to pay its merchants on a timely basis, and that the treasury was nearly depleted. Finding a pretext to speak with two merchants, allegedly to thank them for their services, he was quietly able to verify that the rumors were correct. The pope could see now that appointing Cardinal Casaroli as secretary of state had been a grave error in that the pope had probably let the fox watch the henhouse, undoubtedly the same mistake made by his predecessor, Pope Benedict XIII.

Clement considered reassigning the cardinal to Latin America or Asia, thereby relieving him of all financial oversight and ensuring that contact with his allies within the church would be limited. For a person of his stature, this would be viewed as the equivalent of being fired and exiled. But in order to do this, Clement needed ironclad proof of Casaroli's wrongdoing, so as not to invite retribution from the cardinal's powerful friends. Otherwise, the politically savvy Casaroli would spin the reassignment as the vindictive actions of a jealous and senile old man who was no longer capable of leading the church. The result would be a marginalization of the pope's authority by those within the curia who felt that they had an obligation to protect the Throne of Saint Peter at any cost, subsequently making Clement little more than a figurehead.

For months the pope beseeched God for guidance, asking how to remove Casaroli while at the same time retaining the confidence of those around him. Then on this present day, his prayers were answered by an unlikely source.

Giuseppe Carlino was a mild-mannered Benedictine monk with an aquiline nose, a broad forehead, and a medium build. He had learned accounting while working at his father's business in Milan and later had transferred those skills to the Mezzegra monastery, where he expertly kept the order's financial records. Eventually, his expertise had come to the attention of Cardinal Casaroli, whereupon he had been summoned to work in the Vatican accounting department, where he would report directly to the secretary of state.

Carlino was risk-adverse and always considered the consequences of his decisions before he acted. He'd heard stories of how Cardinal Casaroli dealt with those who did something behind his back and what happened to them when the cardinal's actions became decidedly non-Christian. Therefore, as he approached the papal apartments, his hands were shaking.

Telling the Swiss Guards that he had a critical financial matter to discuss with the pope, he waited for nearly a minute while the two guards discussed whether to let him enter because, in the Vatican hierarchy, he was essentially a nobody. But because the church's monetary crisis was so well known, the two guards decided to let him pass.

Clement was lying in bed, and Carlino startled the pontiff with his approaching footsteps. After apologizing for the interruption, he quickly introduced himself. When the pope asked why he'd come, he blurted out that he believed the secretary of state, along with the Bank of Rizzo, was embezzling large sums of money from the church. The pope sat up, placed a pillow behind his back, and asked the intruder to sit down and explain. Carlino complied and said that several days ago, he had gone to Cardinal Casaroli's office to ask if he knew about a large payment to a tradesman that seemed to be in error. If there hadn't been a mistake, he wanted to tell Casaroli that the church was being charged an exorbitant amount because his father had similar work performed at a third of the price. After knocking on the cardinal's door, he waited for permission to enter. The corridor outside the secretary of state's office was particularly loud and bustling with activity that morning, and he thought he heard the cardinal call to him to enter. But when he opened the door, he found the office deserted. Realizing his mistake, he was about to leave when he saw a stack of vellum pages on the cardinal's desk. Unable to control his curiosity about what the cardinal was working on, he closed the door and began examining the pages. He knew that what he was doing was a sin, he now told Clement, but he couldn't control himself.

It took him only seconds of looking at the pages before him, he said, to realize that he was looking at a ledger that was nearly identical to the master Vatican ledger he maintained, except that the numbers between the two were vastly different. For example, he explained, there were many line items in Cardinal Casaroli's ledger that didn't appear in his. Whereas the Vatican's official financial records indicated that it was losing an enormous amount of money because donations failed to cover the Holy See's expenses and because of the need to pay off the massive debt the previous pontiff had incurred, the cardinal's ledger presented a vastly different picture. It indicated that the papacy had not only adequate cash flow to meet its ongoing expenses but also more than enough cash to retire all outstanding debt.

The pope listened intently to Carlino's story without interrupting, and whenever the monk would pause to give the pontiff an opportunity to ask questions, the pope instead encouraged him to continue.

Carlino went on to explain that there were two reasons for the disparities between the master ledger and the one on the cardinal's desk. The first was the additional line entries, which represented an enormous amount of cash. The second was that the cash the Vatican had received from faithful wealthy donors was far less than the amounts reflected in the cardinal's ledger. The unaccounted-for funds were instead divided between two numbered accounts at the Bank of Rizzo in Milan. In a muted voice, Carlino said that the only explanation for what he had seen was that the secretary of state was, in concert with someone at the Bank of Rizzo, embezzling church funds.

The monk ended his story by telling the pope that after what he'd seen, he had hastily left the cardinal's office and had just closed the door behind him when he saw Casaroli walking down the hall not more than twenty paces from where he stood. Fortunately, the secretary of state did not walk fast, and he was speaking with a thin man with long legs and a short torso. Therefore, the monk's exit had gone unnoticed. Otherwise, he would have had to explain the unexplainable—what he had been doing in the cardinal's office.

Clement's response surprised the monk. He told Carlino to go back to the cardinal's office, take the ledger, and then make two copies of it while in his room. Afterward, he was to document the discrepancies between the cardinal's ledger and the Vatican's master ledger. The pope then told him to send one copy to someone he would trust with his life: that person should be able to both safeguard the ledger without looking at it and return it upon request. The pope went on to say that God had indeed provided the timing for this initiative, in that the cardinal was to depart the next day on a planned trip to Orvieto. Although his journey was ostensibly to visit a cathedral and solicit donations from the wealthy in the area, the pope said that it was an open secret that Casaroli's real reason for going was that the cathedral was close to numerous vineyards whose vintners lavishly entertained the secretary of state.

With a look of relief on his face, the monk kissed the pope's ring and then left.

Carlino returned to the cardinal's office the following day, not long after Casaroli's departure, and in a plan that he'd formulated only hours before, he asked the Swiss Guard patrolling the interior of the administrative building to unlock the cardinal's office so that he could clean the floor. Since clergy routinely did this type of menial work, the guard complied. It took the monk an hour to find where the ledger was hidden, after which he proceeded to clean half the floor until it shined brightly. When he was finished, he put the ledger under his loose-fitting cassock and left.

He spent that night studying what he'd taken and the next couple of days making two copies of Casaroli's ledger. Returning to the cardinal's office three days after he'd taken the ledger, he asked the guard on duty to unlock the door so that he could finish cleaning the floor, since he previously hadn't had time to complete his task. The guard was not the same one Carlino had previously encountered, but he nevertheless unlocked Casaroli's office, looked inside, and saw the disparity in the cleanliness of one half of the floor compared to the other. After the guard left, Carlino returned the ledger to its hiding place and finished polishing the other side of the office.

CHAPTER 4

1740

T HE ELEGANT HORSE-DRAWN carriage raced through the streets of Milan as the coachman's long whip snapped above the heads of the two white horses propelling it. The carriage's single passenger stood six feet four, nearly a foot above the average man. He was thin, with long legs and a short torso. His face, which was hard-bitten and gave the impression that he was always in pain, made him appear menacing and unsympathetic, both of which were accurate.

Duke Federigo Rizzo had ordered the coachman to take him to his bank with all possible haste, which was unusual since it was ten in the evening and the financial institution had long since closed. But the coachman, whose whipping scars on his back were a testament to the duke's intolerance of being questioned, would have sped the horses through the gates of hell if asked.

The carriage had barely pulled to a stop when Rizzo threw open his carriage door and hurried toward the bank's front entrance. The large single-story building was thirty feet tall and encompassed an entire block in the center of the city's financial center. All four sides of the structure had long rows of fluted Doric columns that led to a roof covered with large overlapping marble tiles. The entire structure closely resembled the Parthenon, which had been Rizzo's intent.

The duke opened the door and walked past the five night workers, who stood as he proceeded to his office in the rear of the building. Seated in a chair in front of the duke's desk, in the center of the immense room decorated with dark-stained, heavy furniture, was a gray-haired man of average height and weight. He had the deep-lined face of someone who had suffered adversity for much of his life. The dark circles under Paolo Tolomei's eyes told Federigo Rizzo all he needed to know as he sat down behind his desk.

"I take it, because of the urgency of this meeting, that the news you carry is not good," said Rizzo.

"His Holiness asked that I immediately convey that you are to forthwith return the Vatican's money, according to the entries in Cardinal Casaroli's ledger," Tolomei said.

"Was the cardinal there when you met the pope?" Rizzo asked, seemingly unfazed by what his papal envoy had just said.

"No. I learned from one of my sources that the cardinal was in Orvieto and was ordered by the Holy Father to return to Rome with all haste. Only a monk was present when I met with His Holiness. He's the one who showed me the entries in Cardinal Casaroli's ledger."

"He showed you the ledger?"

Tolomei nodded.

"Did the pope say anything else?"

Tolomei fidgeted. He apparently didn't want to convey what he was about to say, and his voice sounded reluctant as he continued. "I was about to add that His Holiness said that if the money is not returned in a fortnight, he intends to excommunicate you."

Rizzo began to sweat, and his face turned pale. Walking to an empty brass container in the corner of his office, he vomited his early dinner. Tolomei didn't question this reaction, even though the duke was outwardly a practicing Catholic and inwardly an atheist, because it was completely understandable. In an overwhelmingly Catholic country, where the pope had more power than the ruler of Italy, and in a world where Catholicism was rapidly spreading, being excommunicated by the Catholic Church meant social and business ostracization by anyone who was Catholic.

Rizzo wiped his mouth with his silk scarf and then threw it on the floor beside him. After thinking in silence for several minutes, while his papal envoy fidgeted and waited for a response, he approached Tolomei.

"Please return to Rome and tell the pontiff that he'll receive every scudi within a fortnight," Rizzo said, with a look that told Tolomei that just the opposite would happen.

Once the papal envoy was on his way back to Rome, Rizzo went to his desk and wrote a letter to Casaroli. He had two situations to resolve in short order—he must zero out his financial liability to the papacy and end a partnership that had run its course. The letter he'd written to Casaroli would resolve one situation, and the letter he was about to write would resolve the other.

Casaroli was exhausted. He didn't travel well, and it was nearly midnight when he disembarked from his carriage. He was too fat for the seats in papal carriages, which made it difficult to sleep during a journey, and an advanced case of arthritis in his knees made sitting still for an extended period painful. He was in a bad mood as he limped toward the building in which his office was located. He had an idea of the subject matter that the pontiff wanted to discuss with him, thanks to a letter sent by the patriarch, whose messenger had exhausted a string of horses to reach the cardinal before he entered Rome.

Casaroli walked past the saluting Swiss Guards and entered the building, where he remained in his office for thirty minutes before leaving and crossing the courtyard to the adjacent structure, which housed the papal apartments. Inside his cloak he carried a glass container, previously given to him by Duke Federigo Rizzo for use in extraordinary circumstances. This qualified. When Casaroli arrived at the pope's quarters, the two Swiss Guards standing at attention outside his door recognized him, and one immediately broke rank and opened the door.

As the cardinal approached the pope's bedroom, he was wheezing badly, all but announcing his presence. His lungs were failing miserably in oxygenating a body his size, especially since he had just walked up a flight of stairs before crossing this room. Clement was awake and sitting upright in bed, having been awakened by one of his staff who had seen the cardinal's carriage enter the courtyard.

"Your Holiness," Casaroli said, his tone indicating that his greeting was superficial rather than cordial.

"I have two matters which I'd like to discuss," the pontiff said, ignoring any attempt at cordiality and getting straight to the point. "I've come to learn that the Vatican is not as monetarily destitute as I was led to believe. In fact, we seem to have enough capital to not only run our day-to-day operations but also pay our debts. I've also been presented with proof that the source of our financial problems has been the systematic diversion of Vatican cash into two accounts at the Bank of Rizzo. Perhaps you'd like to comment."

Casaroli's face was emotionless, and he didn't reply, having been forewarned by Rizzo. Instead, he segued in another direction in order to carry out his plan. "May I have a sip of tea? My mouth is parched," Casaroli said, knowing that the pope always had a pot of tea on the table next to him.

"As you wish," the pope responded.

"May I also pour you a cup?"

When the pope nodded, Casaroli quickly took a small glass container from under his cloak and removed the cork stopper. He then poured the friar's cap poison into the pope's cup before pouring his tea. What he was about to give the pontiff came from a tall plant with blue blossoms that grew on the rocky slopes of the mountains to the north. There was no antidote. Death would occur in anywhere from ten minutes to a few hours, depending on the amount ingested. Casaroli used only a small amount of the substance, so that death would summon the pontiff very slowly. Casaroli needed Clement to be alive when he left.

"Your tea, Holiness," Casaroli said as he placed the cup in front of Clement. He watched the pontiff take a sip before speaking again. "I confess, Holy Father, that most of the cardinals who elected you, myself included, believed you to be a year or two from death at that time. This is, of course, why you became pope. Your greatest weakness has been your blind trust of your brethren, the same weakness displayed by your predecessor. This has allowed me to enrich myself and groom your successor."

The pope took a second sip of tea. His facial expression relayed that he hadn't expected Casaroli to be as straightforward as he was. "Your final days in this life will be spent in jail alongside your partner, who I demanded return the money you both stole from the church. I'm going to excommunicate both you and Duke Rizzo." Clement, apparently feeling nauseous, put his hand to his mouth and abruptly ended their conversation by telling the cardinal to leave and make his peace with God.

Upon Casaroli's departure, one of the Swiss Guards entered Clement's bedroom. "May I get you anything, Holy Father?" the guard asked.

"Nothing now. I'm tired and need some sleep."

The Swiss Guard snapped to attention, did an about-face, and left the pope's bedroom. That was the last conversation anyone had with Pope Clement XII.

CHAPTER 5

Present day

WHEN GISMONDI RETURNED at first light, he climbed down to the Fiat at the bottom of the mountain, lying in a flat gravelly area that had once been a riverbed. The vehicle had been reduced to not much more than a crushed shell when it finally impacted the valley floor. The diminutive assassin saw that Salvatore Bruno was lying a hundred feet away and that his black Floto Firenze briefcase, which the patriarch also had but in brown, was an arm's length from him.

Gismondi took a pair of latex gloves from his back pocket and put them on before he picked up the heavy briefcase and tried to open it. But the clasp refused to budge. Not wanting to disturb Bruno's body to try to find the key, he took out his pocketknife and deftly pried open the lock. Expecting to see two ledgers within, he was surprised when he instead saw a thick book on Vatican art and paintings, a package of mints, and a pair of reading glasses.

Duke Rodolfo Rizzo had inherited his family's genetic traits of long lanky legs, a short torso, and above-average height. At six feet, six inches tall, the clean-shaven seventy-one-year-old chairman of the Bank of Rizzo had short gray hair that he combed straight back, close-set blue eyes, and a fleshy nose. He didn't own a pair of jeans, shorts, or casual clothing of any type. Instead, his usual attire was a dark blue Vanquish II suit, a white shirt, a red tie, and black wing tips, all made by Brioni, with each outfit costing as much as a midsize BMW. He was neither fat nor skinny, and his voice was deep and resonant, much like that of the actor Sam Elliott. He was addicted to double espressos, without milk or sugar, and Cohiba's 1966 Edicion Limitada 2011 cigars, both of which he indulged in throughout the day. He was rarely addressed as "Duke" by those who knew him, although he didn't object to the noble title. Instead, most called him "Patriarch," a term of power, nobility, and deference that had clung to the head of the Rizzo family throughout the centuries.

He had married in his late thirties but now had been a widower for nearly fifteen years, his wife of seventeen years having died in a car accident that he'd orchestrated after discovering she'd been too casual in her conversations about his business dealings. He had one son, who was now attending the École Normale Superieure in Paris, where he'd just received a PhD in computer science and was finishing his final semester for a master's degree in economics. They were close, and the heir apparent was intimately familiar with his family's licit and illicit activities and was looking forward to carrying on the family tradition, although he was unaware that his father had arranged for his mother's death.

The patriarch lived on an enormous ancestral estate in the Italian town of Bellagio, which had a breathtaking view of Lake Como, a pristine body of water of glacial origin forty miles from Milan. His property comprised the entire mountain and was valued, according to the tax assessor, at just over five hundred million euros. The top of the mountain had been leveled in the eighteenth century and a residence constructed, although the original structure had been magnitudes smaller than the 150,000 square feet of the current mansion. Beneath the enormous structure was a thirty-car underground private garage for his car collection, along with a separate parking area for an additional hundred vehicles. Both entrances had subsurface heating to keep them free of snow and ice during the winter. Down the mountain and out of sight of the mansion were two greenhouses; three caretaker buildings, which were used as apartments for the staff, who doubled as his security team; and four guesthouses, each with a floor space of approximately three thousand square feet.

One approached the mansion by way of a mile-long private road, protected by two massive ten-foot-high wrought iron gates with security cameras mounted on top of the support posts. A call box positioned several car lengths before this imposing barrier was used to gain entry to the estate. The road, which also was heated in the winter to ward off ice and snow, led to a gravel driveway that was as long as a football field and half that wide, with a divider of ornamental trees and shrubbery down its center.

Perhaps the most magnificent area of the residence was its chapel, which protruded from the north end of the mansion. The five-thousand-square-foot rectangular enclosure, with a three-story-high turret at the far end, boasted fourteen faceted stained-glass windows depicting the Stations of the Cross, seven to a side, extending from the mansion to the turret. In the center of the turret was a circular stained-glass window depicting the resurrection of Christ. The interior of the chapel was strikingly odd in that there were no pews, only a singular, thickly padded black leather chair facing a raised solid gold altar flanked on either side by a gold angel with hands outstretched toward it. High above the interior was a thirty-foot fan vault ceiling overlooking the black marble floor below.

The duke was in his office, which was near the chapel, when Gismondi entered. The office was forty feet long, with a floor of antique oak planks, though a thick gold and black Persian carpet covered all but a two-foot perimeter of floor on all sides. A Louis XIV desk was situated in the center of the room. The wall to the left consisted of a floor-to-ceiling glass window that provided a commanding view of the lake and town. Like all the exterior glass on the residence, it was bulletproof.

Rizzo was expressionless as he sat behind his desk, occasionally flicking an ash from his cigar into a small silver tray as he patiently listened to his assassin, who sat in the straight-backed chair to the left of the patriarch's desk. Gismondi reported that he'd thoroughly searched Salvatore Bruno's home and office, as well as the briefcase he'd carried with him to his death. He'd also gone through the home of the now dead informant. The ledgers were nowhere to be found. Rizzo's day didn't get any better when Gismondi told him that the front of his $285,000 Holland & Holland Range Rover had been damaged while forcing Bruno's car off the road, and a piece of the front grille was missing.

"Bruno's son will be arriving today or tomorrow," said Rizzo. "I want you to return to the crash site and place the briefcase exactly where you found it. But first, I'm going to put some papers inside."

Gismondi looked confused.

"As I previously explained, my internet search indicated that Mauro Bruno is a remarkable detective, which is why I needed his father's death to look like an accident. It's also why I want him searching for the ledgers. There's no telling where his father may have hidden them. But his son just may know. But to expose that hiding place, I have to motivate him to search for the ledgers."

"I mean this with all due respect, but isn't that dangerous? What if he finds the ledgers and then gives them to the authorities before we can stop him?"

"Because you and the men I'm assigning to you are going to keep him under tight surveillance, starting the moment he sets foot in Milan, and you will grab the ledgers as soon as he finds them. You're also going to make sure he doesn't have an opportunity to give them to anyone. Since he'll probably stay at his father's residence, place cameras inside and post someone outside the residence as well. Then stake out the train and bus stations and both airports since we don't know how he'll travel from Venice to Milan. You can get Mauro Bruno's picture off the internet."

"And when we get the ledgers?"

"Kill Bruno and anyone else who may have seen them. I need the entire team focused on this—which is why I want you to take Sartori with you."

Those last words brought about a look of disapproval. Davide Sartori technically worked for Gismondi, and it should have been up to the patriarch's top assassin to pick his team—not that Gismondi or anyone else would say that to the patriarch. But it was well known that Sartori, a former hit man for the mafia, didn't like to work for anyone except the *capo dei capi*, or boss of all bosses, which made his relationship with Gismondi substantially less than perfect. The fact that

Sartori had an ego bigger than most Hollywood celebrities also didn't help. This opinion of himself had been formed when he left the mafia for Rizzo's security team, which had been allowed to happen only because his boss owed the patriarch a substantial favor. Generally, transfers out of the mafia were discouraged by a bullet. Putting Gismondi and Sartori together was a message from the patriarch to Gismondi: find the ledgers, or he was standing next to his replacement.

CHAPTER 6

I T WAS EIGHT in the evening when Chief Inspector Mauro Bruno stepped off the train at Milan's central train station. In his late forties, the five feet eleven detective had salt-and-pepper hair combed straight back, a neatly trimmed black mustache with flecks of gray, piercing brown eyes, and a waistline that showed he was ten pounds heavier than his ideal weight. He was not comfortable wearing casual clothing, preferring instead to present the formal appearance that he believed was in keeping with his job title of chief inspector. Therefore, he always went to work in one of his three identical dark blue suits, all of which were worn and shiny with age, but which he pressed each morning to maintain a neat appearance. His shirt color was always white, and his ties light blue, because his late mother had told him that combination went well with his suit and made him look distinguished.

The two-and-a-half-mile taxi ride to his father's Porta Romana residence, southeast of the city center, took thirteen minutes. The area was a collection of nineteenth- and early-twentieth-century buildings, generally no more than half a dozen stories high, interspersed with pocket residential neighborhoods, each composed of a dozen or so individual homes. The white-brick villa in front of which the taxi stopped stood on a street that ran parallel to the main thoroughfare. Between the two was a row of stout trees and five-foot-high bushes. Directly across from Salvatore Bruno's residence, and accessed through a large gap in the bushes, was a small park edged with the same type of trees and bushes that bordered the street.

The Venetian detective paid the taxi driver, opened the six-foot-high wrought iron gate that guarded the driveway, and walked the twenty yards to the front door. He inserted the key his father had once given him and walked through the small entrance hall and into a living room, to the side of which was a diminutive garden. The villa had no security system and only the most basic of door locks, which had always been a subject of contention between father and son when Mauro came to visit. Amazingly, in the forty years his father had lived here, ten since his mother died, there'd never been a break-in—until now. The living room had been ransacked, the contents of drawers emptied onto the floor. Padded chairs were slit, and couch cushions were cut. The rest of the residence, Mauro found on inspection, had received similar treatment. Whatever the intruders had been looking for, it wasn't valuables—because his father's iPad, Apple laptop computer, and even silver serving pieces were lying on the floor.

Bruno picked up the two serving pieces, which were brightly polished. The two small circular plates, each eight inches in diameter, had been a wedding gift to his parents from a relative who was close to his mother. His father had told him that these were his mother's favorite possessions since the person who had given them the pieces died of cancer not long after their wedding. His father had later learned that the relative knew she had only months to live and gave them the pieces so that they would think of her when she was gone. Bruno put the two pieces on the kitchen counter. He was about to call the police but stopped since there was little that they'd be able to do, other than write a report and file it, since he didn't know if anything had been taken. The fact that the intruders might not have found what they were after and might believe that Bruno knew the whereabouts of whatever they were looking for didn't escape him.

It was early morning, and Sartori was relieving himself behind a bush not far from the duke's Chevrolet Suburban, which was parked across the street from Salvatore Bruno's white-brick residence. Yesterday Sartori had placed wireless video cameras with night-vision capabilities throughout the house and since then had waited for the eventual arrival of Mauro Bruno. The call reporting that Bruno was on his way from the train station had come from one of the duke's minions, who'd spotted the Venetian detective as he was walking toward a taxi.

Nothing much had happened after the detective arrived at the house, other than his show of understandable surprise that the place had been ransacked. Interestingly, however, he didn't call the police. Instead, he looked around the residence, picked a couple of items up off the floor, and then went to bed. The fact that Sartori had been stuck looking at the digital camera feed of someone sleeping all night, while that stick-thin prima donna he technically worked for slept in a warm bed, did not sit well with him. But Sartori couldn't countermand the duke's orders to follow Gismondi's instructions. What he needed was an opportunity to discredit his nemesis in the eyes of the patriarch or else help him meet his end in the confusion of battle. He was mulling over how he could bring about that second scenario as he pulled up his zipper and started back toward his vehicle.

At that moment, Bruno stepped out of the front door of the residence and lit a cigarette. Fortunately for Sartori, he wasn't in the Suburban when the chief inspector blew out a puff of smoke and looked closely at it; otherwise, they'd have been staring directly at each other. Sartori, seeing this, mumbled to himself in Italian about being an imbecile for not considering that a detective with Bruno's reputation, at least from what the patriarch had said about him, would notice the anomaly of such a large car on a street filled with compact vehicles. That made it useless for surveillance.

Sartori crouched down behind the bush and placed a call to one of the security staff at the duke's estate, telling him to bring his personal vehicle to the stakeout as quickly as possible. Forty minutes later, a Volkswagen Golf parked down the street, and he exchanged keys with the driver.

Chief Inspector Mauro Bruno was not a late sleeper, routinely getting up, even on weekends, at 5:30 a.m. Today was no exception. After he showered, shaved, and put on fresh clothing, he walked outside and had his first cigarette since getting off the train. His coworkers referred to them as cancer sticks, and he didn't disagree. He knew that God had given him only one set of lungs and that smoking an average of twenty cigarettes a day was a prescription for emphysema and several other maladies that he was too scared to inquire about. But he'd been addicted since becoming a police officer at the age of twenty-two and found that smoking lowered the stress that came with the job. Over time he had realized that he needed to rid himself of this dependency or suffer health consequences later in life. He had tried hypnosis, patches, and even prescription drugs, but nothing seemed to work. So far, he'd been lucky. His last physical had shown that he was slightly overweight but cancer-free.

He took one last puff and then threw the cigarette butt over the gate. On the other side of the street were several open parking spaces, something seldom seen in Rome, Florence, or even the areas of Venice where cars were permitted. Even more unusual was the Suburban SUV that was parked below a canopy of trees. Anything that size would have virtually no chance of finding a large enough parking space in those other cities unless it was inside a parking garage, and even then it was a toss-up as to whether the owner would have to purchase two spaces.

Walking back into the house, Bruno found a box of Raisin Bran cereal on the kitchen floor and some milk in the refrigerator. Following breakfast, he made himself a cup of espresso. Yesterday he'd spoken to the undertaker, who had said that he could come by at 10:00 a.m. to see his father and sign the necessary papers for his entombment in the family mausoleum. But before that he wanted to visit the accident site and get a perspective on what had happened. It was not that he didn't believe it had been an accident; he'd driven that road before with his father and found it to be exceedingly treacherous. But he needed to see where his father had died in order to get closure.

After leaving the rental car lot in his Fiat Grande Punto, Bruno wove his way through a dozen city streets and eventually entered the A9 highway, which led to the Lake Como region. Once on the thoroughfare, he headed toward Mezzegra and the narrow strip of land that traversed the mountain range near the town. It had been twenty-five years since he'd been on this narrow dirt road, which could more aptly be described as a path since Roman soldiers had carved it out more than a millennium ago. Driving on this treacherous dirt corridor didn't bring back fond memories because every time he had accompanied his father on this road, Mauro would end up reciting Hail Marys and Our Fathers until they finally entered the highway in the valley below. The reason for this was that his father had seemed to ignore the narrowness of the path and the nonadhesion of the tires to the soft dirt, carrying on a conversation as if they were driving on a city street and turning his head toward Mauro from time to time when making a point.

Fifty yards before the hairpin turn, Bruno stopped his vehicle and walked to where the road made a ninety-degree turn. The chief inspector expected a single set of tire tracks or skid marks that went to the edge and over. But what he saw instead was a myriad of tire tracks embedded in the soft dirt a short distance from the drop. It initially seemed reasonable to assume that these belonged to police vehicles and other first responders because there was still only one set of tracks, better described as troughs in the soft dirt, that went all the way to the edge. Unexplainably, however, one set of tracks that Bruno initially assumed to be from first responders ran perpendicular to the edge, almost as if the driver hadn't seen the hairpin turn and had stopped just before driving off the mountain. It was consistent with what one might see if one car pushed another off the cliff. Bruno removed his cell phone from his pocket and took photos of the area.

The chief inspector cautiously walked to the lip of the cliff and looked over. At the very bottom of the mountain was a raft of debris that had ripped off the vehicle as it made its way to the riverbed below. His father, according to the officer who had phoned Bruno in Venice, had been thrown from his car and landed in the riverbed not far from it.

As Bruno was about to return to his car, he saw the sun reflect off something in the knee-high brush to his left. It was barely exposed. Reaching down and pulling the object out of the brush, he saw that it was a jagged piece of chrome that seemed to have come from the front grille of a vehicle. Since the chrome was still very shiny, it couldn't have been exposed to the elements for very long. Even though there were no markings on the six-by-four-inch piece, the fact that it was chrome and not plastic meant that it had come from a luxury vehicle. It also meant that an insurance company or individual was going to be writing a large check to replace it.

He carried the jagged chrome back to his car and continued down the dirt road until he came to a turnoff, eventually finding his way to the riverbed and the crash site. The area of impact wasn't hard to find because the crash had created a scarred section of riverbed that contrasted sharply with the area surrounding it. Looking up at the extensive debris from the car that clung to the mountain, Bruno could see that the Fiat must have somersaulted down the cliff during some part of its journey in order to lay down the debris field above him. In over two decades of police work, he'd seen innumerable crash sites and bodies and every conceivable method of brutality that one person or group could inflict on another. And even though he had felt empathy for all those killed, injured, or aggrieved parties, nothing had ever tugged at his heart as much as seeing where his father's life had come to an end. He thought back to his childhood and his father holding him by the hand and walking him down a dry riverbed such as this, in search of whatever fruit or berry they might find in the wild. Those days hadn't been so much about what they found as about the adventure of searching for something together. Those Sundays had become fond memories for both, and Bruno wished he'd savored each one a little more at the time. Tears gently fell from both his eyes as he finally realized that he'd lost the last member of his family and his best friend. After standing in silence for a while, Bruno removed his cell phone from his jacket pocket and began taking photos of the area around him.

CHAPTER 7

I T WAS ALMOST eleven when Bruno entered the coroner's office, where he signed the necessary forms to transfer his father's body to a funeral home and take possession of his personal items, including his briefcase. He was then escorted to a private room where, five minutes later, the body was wheeled in on a gurney. Left alone by the morgue staff, he pulled the white sheet covering the body up to his father's neck—an automatic response to keep him warm in the cold room.

The body displayed less facial trauma than one might expect from someone who had been propelled through a window and had then tumbled down a mountain to a gravelly riverbed, although the coroner had mentioned that almost every bone below Salvatore Bruno's neck was broken, shattered, or cracked. Mauro, who would later tell the coroner that he was glad that his last vision of his dad wasn't as horrific as he originally had expected, stood beside his role model and best friend and, for some unknown reason, thought back to the day he had informed his parents that he was moving to Venice. For his father, who had expected his son to raise a family in Milan and to perhaps, with Salvatore's help, buy the house up the street, this had the same emotional impact as a

45

brick hitting a thin glass window. But when Mauro explained that the reason for the move was that he'd fallen in love with a *vigili urbani*—a municipal police officer who worked in administration—his father had said that he understood. His mother, who was now presented with the possibility of having grandchildren, had been overjoyed. Loving their son deeply, neither parent wanted to question how their son had fallen in love so deeply after being in Venice only a week. It was only later, during a family discussion, that both admitted to him that they'd decided to trust his judgment and let nature take its course.

Mauro had met Katarina, his future wife, at a Venice bar during a trip to the famed city just after college, a graduation gift from his parents. There was instant chemistry between them, and later that night, he went home with her. The attraction between them continued to grow to the point where they decided to live together. Both knew that meant that he'd have to relocate to Venice.

Once he got settled in Venice, his future wife suggested that he might like to become a police officer. Since law bored him, and the idea of making a positive impact on the community seemed appealing, he decided to explore the vocation, although he was more interested in the Polizia di Stato, which had a wider investigative and jurisdictional umbrella, than in the municipal police. He first turned to his father for advice, as he'd done so often in his life, and the senior Bruno had several discussions with his son. Mauro's father told him flat-out that corporate or legal work wasn't going to make him happy. Instead, helping others and protecting the weak seemed to fit more with the personality of the man he'd seen grow to adulthood. He therefore encouraged Mauro to apply to the state police, just as he wanted, and gave him a strong letter of reference.

The younger Bruno was accepted to the academy and passed its rigorous training program with ease. Less than a year later, he and Katarina were married. But the union lasted only one year: the love of his life was killed by an intruder who broke into their Venice home and killed Bruno's wife and unborn child while he was on night duty. The murderer was never found. Bruno was startled back to the present from that awful day, twenty-two years ago next month, when the door behind him opened and the coroner entered the room.

"The funeral home driver will be here in about two hours," said the coroner, a man of medium height in his early seventies with gray hair and a fleshy face that came from being fifty pounds overweight. "I'm sorry for your loss. Your father was a good man, loved and respected by all who worked with him. I can say with certainty that in the ten years I had the privilege to work with him, there wasn't a time we were together that he didn't brag about you."

"Thank you," Bruno said.

The men spoke a few minutes longer before the coroner turned to leave. As he approached the door, he stopped and turned toward Bruno.

"It's a shame you don't work in Milan. The police could use your help to solve the five murders that occurred in the city yesterday."

"Five murders in one day, not counting my father?"

"That's correct. But your father's death was an accident, not a homicide."

"How were the five victims killed?"

"An elderly gentleman was murdered by someone who put a knife into his brain. The mayor was shot on the front steps of city hall, with the gunman apparently taking the shot from the elderly man's apartment, which was an astonishing thousand yards away. So those two murders are connected. The third and fourth homicides were of an abbot and a librarian at the Benedictine monastery in Mezzegra. They were killed at close range with a handgun. The fifth homicide was that of your father's deputy. He was strangled in his home by an intruder."

"My father, his deputy, and the mayor were all senior government officials. There must be a connection between the three, even though you believe my father's death was an accident. If someone looks hard enough, they will probably find that the two murders at the monastery are connected to the other three."

"As I said, it's a shame you don't work in Milan."

"How many detectives are assigned to these murders?"

"One, as far as I know—Inspector Elia Donati of the state police."

"Perhaps I should give him a call."

"Do that. But you should be aware that he has a large ego and believes that his judgments are infallible, or at least that's my experience. You should also note that he's been seen, from time to time, going to the patriarch's estate."

"The patriarch—Duke Rodolfo Rizzo, the wealthiest man in Italy. It seems odd that they'd have anything in common or that they'd move in the same social circle."

"More likely there's a monetary reason for their conversations, although Elia's father is quite wealthy. Perhaps there's enough blue in the family blood for the patriarch to socialize with him. Now that I think about it, at one time I did hear talk that your father was trying to determine if the junior Donati was on the take, but the inspector seems to have expertly covered his trail, and there were never any findings of corruption."

"*Grazie mille*," Bruno said. He then kissed his father on the forehead and left with the small cardboard box containing his dad's personal items.

Walking outside the morgue, he sat down on a bench and lit a cigarette, then opened the box and looked at its contents. Besides his father's Floto Firenze briefcase, which had been an anniversary gift from his mother, the box contained clothes, a wallet, and three keys—one to the residence, one to his briefcase, and the other to the long-dead Fiat Panda. Looking closely at the briefcase, he saw scratches around the locks that were not dissimilar from what one might see if they'd been picked. But when he tried to open the briefcase, he found it locked and needed the key to gain entry.

Inside were a pair of reading glasses, a small package of mints, and five pieces of paper. Taking out the pages, Bruno saw that the first was a note to the mayor from an unknown informant. It indicated that the informant had documentation of corruption within the government, which he'd accumulated in two massive loose-leaf ledgers. As proof the person had enclosed three photocopies of bank statements that were purportedly from these ledgers. The name of the account holder, the name of the bank, and the account number were redacted on each statement. The note went on to explain that in return for handing over this information, the informant wanted half the money from these offshore accounts. In addition, he wanted to be placed in the country's witness protection program. Once he received a signed agreement memorializing these terms, he'd turn over both ledgers.

The last sheet of paper was a letter from the mayor to Bruno's father indicating that he had granted the informant's requests and that in return he'd received two binders, each containing a ledger. Given the corruption indicated by the informant, the mayor requested that his chief prosecutor personally protect the ledgers until they were needed for detailed examination and verification.

After reading these pages and examining the tire tracks and broken car grille on the mountain road, and with two decades–plus of investigative instinct, Bruno concluded that his father's death probably wasn't an accident and was linked to the other deaths. Moreover, whoever had killed all these people wanted these ledgers. The break-in at his father's home, which Bruno initially had believed to be a random robbery or the result of someone hearing of Salvatore Bruno's death and deciding to rob the place, had instead been a search for these two books. That assumption seemed to be confirmed when Bruno noticed on his way to the site of his father's accident that someone was following him—possibly the same person who had installed the wireless cameras in the senior Bruno's home, which he'd seen upon searching the ransacked residence. It also meant that whoever was behind this believed that the son would know where his father would hide something of such importance. As it turned out, that assumption too was entirely correct.

Bruno was known among his colleagues for being meticulous. This meant that even the smallest detail in an investigation received the same level of scrutiny as any other detail. Therefore, in determining what vehicle the chrome grille had come from, the chief inspector decided to do an internet search on his cell phone for all the luxury car dealerships in the city. He decided to eliminate those selling sports cars and focus instead on the larger luxury sedans since sports cars didn't usually come out on the winning end of collisions. If a car had pushed his father's Fiat off the road, it had probably been a larger vehicle.

He started with Mercedes, then went to BMW and Bentley, continuing down the list based on how geographically close the dealerships were to one another so that he could cover the maximum number in the shortest amount of time. None of the dealerships' staff recognized the section of grille presented to them until he showed it to the maintenance manager at the Range Rover dealership, along with his Polizia di Stato creds. Asking Bruno to follow him, the manager walked to the maintenance bay and pointed to a deep green Range Rover with a gaping hole in the front grille. The manager didn't need to consult the maintenance logs in the computer because he had been present when the damaged SUV was brought in—the morning after Salvatore Bruno's death—and since only forty of this particular model of Range Rover were produced per year, he had no trouble recalling that the owner was Duke Rodolfo Rizzo.

CHAPTER 8

1740

I T WAS EARLY in the morning, and there was a sharp bite of coldness in the air when Carlino greeted the young Benedictine monk who approached him on horseback. The Vatican accountant had woken up the eighteen-year-old less than an hour ago, to inform him that he was being sent to a monastery in the north and would not return to the Vatican. He was to take his possessions, which essentially meant his clothing and Bible, and saddle a horse from the stables. Carlino didn't explain his actions. The younger monk had taken an oath of obedience and was expected to follow the directions of his superiors without question.

As the young monk approached, Carlino handed him a heavy brown satchel bearing the Vatican seal. Inside were two hollowed-out leather-bound books, duplicating the hiding place where Carlino had found the ledger in the cardinal's office. One book contained a copy of the ledger from Cardinal Casaroli's office, and the other was a duplicate of the one from the Vatican accounting department.

Once the satchel was secured to the saddle, Carlino handed the monk a pouch stuffed with food, several canteens of water, and a map to the monastery, on which was written the name of the abbot to whom the monk was to deliver the satchel. Last, Carlino handed the young monk a sealed letter to present to the abbot, requesting, on behalf of the pope, that the abbot hide both books in a location that wouldn't inspire curiosity, but where they could be easily accessed and returned to the Vatican when requested. The monk took the letter and placed it deep inside his clothing, and after Carlino led them in prayer, he set his horse off at a gallop.

Three weeks later, the librarian at the Benedictine monastery in Mezzegra was handed two books by the abbot, with instructions to store them within the monastery's library, in a location known only to the librarian and in a place that would be impossible for another monk to see or access. The librarian responded at once that he had the perfect location. Once the abbot left, the librarian moved a ladder to a corner bookshelf, climbed to the highest rung, ten feet above the floor, and placed both books behind a pillar. There they could be seen only by someone standing less than a foot away. Although curious about the subject matter of the untitled books, the librarian respected the abbot's desire for secrecy and didn't open either volume. Eight months later, the librarian contracted pneumonia and died. Another monk assumed his position, not knowing anything about the books that had been handed to his predecessor by the abbot, who in turn did not think to ask if the new librarian had any idea of the location of the books entrusted to the monastery because he had his own health problems. Several months later, the abbot also passed away.

It was early morning when Cardinal Ettore Casaroli heard the pounding on the door of his apartment. Opening it, he was saluted by two Swiss Guards. The cardinal was already fully dressed because he had been expecting their arrival. He nodded to the two stern-looking men, one of whom requested that he follow them to the papal quarters. No explanation was offered, and none requested, because the cardinal already knew why they'd come.

Much like the military, the clergy had a chain of command and defined courses of action to take should various situations arise. Therefore, when the person who brought Clement his breakfast had found the pope dead, he had summoned the prefect of the papal household, who, after visually verifying that the pope was no longer with the living, had sent for the camerlengo of the Holy Roman Church—a position also held by Casaroli. Among his other responsibilities within the Vatican, the camerlengo was the one who officially verified, in the presence of others who would also be summoned according to tradition, the pontiff's death. He was also the person tasked with issuing the death certificate.

When Casaroli arrived at the papal apartments, four men were standing around Clement's bed: the master of papal liturgical ceremonies, who was responsible for the smooth enactment of rituals with regard to the pope; the secretary and chancellor of the Apostolic Camera, both of whom were bishops and part of the government of the Papal States; and the pontiff's physician, who resided in the Vatican and had already determined that the pope was dead. As Casaroli approached the body, the master of papal liturgical ceremonies handed him a small silver hammer.

"Lorenzo, *dormisne*?" the camerlengo asked, addressing Clement by his baptismal name and inquiring if he was sleeping as he lightly tapped Clement's forehead, as custom dictated, with the silver hammer. Casaroli repeated this ritual twice more. When he received no response, he said,

"I declare that His Holiness Pope Clement XII is truly dead." Casaroli genuflected, with the assistance of the two bishops, while the others in the room knelt, as he read Psalm 130. Following this, he removed the pontiff's ring and smashed it with the hammer to symbolize the end of Clement's reign and to prevent someone from forging a document using his seal. Once this was done, Casaroli ordered everyone to leave and ordered the Swiss Guards to lock and seal the door to the papal quarters. This was ostensibly done, according to tradition, to prevent looting by the staff and members of the curia, which had been a common occurrence in past papacies. But Casaroli had a separate reason for doing this—he wanted to return later and thoroughly search for the financial information that Clement apparently had been given. No one could dispute his commands because from now until a successor pope was elected, he would be considered the acting pontiff.

Whatever confidence Casaroli had that he would find the financial documents in the papal apartments vanished after his second search of Clement's quarters. Since Clement was blind, the ledgers would have been brought here and read to the pontiff by someone who had direct access to the apostolic accounting function. If that person hadn't left them here, Casaroli reasoned that the person still must have them. The list of who that might be was short, and he was determined to interrogate each person until he discovered who had betrayed him.

As Casaroli walked back to his office, his limp was worse, the search of the papal apartments having placed a great deal of strain on his knees. He needed to sit down. As he approached his office, he put his hand in his pocket to retrieve his key but then remembered that he'd left it in his quarters. Fortunately, a guard was nearby, and Casaroli summoned him to open the door. Walking to his chair, he nearly slipped but grabbed the desk just in time to keep himself from falling. Looking at the floor, he saw that it was spotless and highly polished. Although the most junior members of the clergy were charged with housekeeping chores, he'd never had someone take this much care. Even though he had a hundred things on his mind—from planning Clement's funeral to the conclave to finding the leak within his organization that had forced him to kill the pope—somehow rewarding the person who hadn't settled for mediocrity took the top spot for his immediate attention.

He summoned the guard and asked if he knew which of the clergy had cleaned his office. As it happened, this guard had been on patrol the day the monk had asked to clean the remainder of the office, and although he didn't know the monk's name, the description he provided the acting head of the Vatican was just as good: it sounded like Giuseppe Carlino. Disappointed at what he'd heard, because one of the perks of working in accounting was that the staff was exempt from all menial work, Casaroli dismissed the guard and went to the shelf on the wall behind his desk, where he removed a hollowed-out book. Opening it, he saw that the string around the bundle of pages was tied slightly differently from his usual method—something he wouldn't have noticed if he hadn't already been suspicious. Slamming the book on his desk, he had no doubt that he'd found his traitor.

When Ettore Casaroli opened the door to the accounting office and entered, the six clergymen sitting at their desks stood and bowed their heads as a sign of respect to the acting pope. Turning to Carlino, Casaroli asked that the monk accompany him. He didn't say where they were going or why he needed him, but it was a request the monk couldn't refuse.

Although it was not yet noon, the dense cloud cover created the illusion that it was much later in the day as the two men left the building in which Carlino worked and headed toward a section of the Vatican used by the church's support staff and various trades. Casaroli's limp was, despite the two canes he was using to take the pressure off his feet, steadily becoming worse. In addition, the overweight cardinal wheezed continually during their journey as his lungs tried to suck in every molecule of air that they could to power his massive frame. After walking by the stables and past the grain warehouses and mill, they were now in an area of the Vatican that the monk had never seen. Carlino's apprehension grew and eventually transitioned to outright fear because the cardinal still hadn't said a word, even though the monk had tried several times to engage him in conversation.

Thirty minutes after it began, their journey appeared to end when the cardinal opened the front door of a one-story pitched-roof wooden structure that appeared to be an abandoned dwelling. There was no furniture inside the structure, and the floors and walls were warped from age and moisture. Although very little light was able to enter the dwelling through its two windows, a room in the back was lit by the flickering glow of two lanterns, both of which were visible from the front door. Casaroli led the way toward the light and was the first to enter the room. As soon as Carlino set foot in the room, he was attacked by two men, who bound and gagged him.

Still not saying a word, the cardinal unlocked and opened the singular door on the right side of the room, which led to a descending stairway. Abandoning his canes, he grabbed a lantern off the floor and followed Carlino and his two escorts down a long flight of stairs.

One didn't have to descend far to smell mold and stale moist air, which increased exponentially the deeper one went. The stairs ended at a large stone-faced room that was dimly lit with lanterns. The rectangular basement carried the additional scent of urine and feces from an open-pit latrine in the corner. Carlino, who initially had no idea what he was being led to, tried desperately to pull away from his escorts when he saw the row of devices that were clearly meant to inflict massive amounts of pain. Opposite them, on the other side of the stone-lined chamber, were three prison cells measuring six by eight feet, their iron bars long ago oxidized into an orange-red-brown color. Anyone who entered this chamber and looked at the devices would logically draw only one conclusion—that they'd soon confess to anything their torturer wanted to hear.

The cardinal wasn't a fan of torture. In fact, the sight of blood or gore made him nauseous. As a result, he seldom witnessed what went on in the chamber. But in this situation he had to make an exception because he needed to find out everything the monk knew about his financial dealings and to whom he'd given this information besides Clement. The men who usually extracted information on his behalf, although loyal to him, would be sent away when the cardinal asked the monk these questions, and once he'd extracted what he felt to be the truth, the monk would be killed.

With an imperious wave of his hand, Casaroli signaled for the torture to begin, whereupon one of the guards grabbed the monk, ripped off his clothes, and placed him in the first device. Within seconds, as the iron spikes penetrated his skin, the sound of his screams reflected off the chamber's stone interior. And so it began.

Seven hours after it started, it was over. The monk was dead. During his ordeal he had verified time and again that he'd told only Clement about the financial irregularities. Casaroli was inclined to accept that story because he firmly believed that no one could withstand intense torture without eventually telling the truth.

CHAPTER 9

CARDINAL CASAROLI HAD always been a strategist, carefully planning whose ring he should kiss as he made his way up the liturgical hierarchy, until he eventually had become the person whose ring everyone, save for one person, wanted to place their lips on. He had survived numerous attempts to destroy his career, had formed partnerships with anyone who could advance his agenda and make him money, and was extremely astute at reading people and understanding their motivations. The letter he'd received from Duke Rizzo as he was returning from Orvieto, warning him that the pope knew of their embezzlement of church funds, had indirectly told him that their sixteen-year partnership was at an end.

The letter had begun innocently enough, instructing him to kill Clement with a poison that the duke had given him some time ago. He didn't have an issue with murdering the pontiff; Clement needed to die so that Casaroli and the other members of his group could put a malleable successor on the throne. The fact that the pope had learned of his embezzlement merely accelerated the date of the pontiff's departure from this life. What unsettled Casaroli was the fact that the duke had directed him to cease any further appropriation of church funds and assets and to destroy all records documenting their activities. So it wasn't logical to conclude that their business would resume after the pope's death, especially since there had been no mention of future business dealings. And knowing the duke as well as he did, the cardinal also believed that these instructions were but the first steps Rizzo would take to protect himself and his fortune. Casaroli's now former partner had ended all his previous business relationships by killing the other party. He didn't believe he'd be the exception to that practice.

The cardinal wasn't nearly as wealthy as Duke Rizzo because he had a habit of gambling, and he was terrible at cards and every other game of chance. This had put a significant dent in his wealth. But he still had enough money that he could retire in South America, where the winters were warm and no one would know or care about his past. The problem was getting his money out of the Bank of Rizzo without creating suspicion. Although he had some cash, most of his wealth was in investments in which the duke had placed him. Asking the duke to liquidate these ventures could very well accelerate his death. Thus, the strategist in him realized that he needed an insurance policy that would guarantee his longevity.

Taking a sheet of stationery from the corner of his desk, he wrote a confession detailing the theft of several irreplaceable church relics that he and the duke had stolen, along with a full accounting of the pair's embezzlement. He took this, the letter the duke had written him, and both the fake and accurate ledgers, and placed them in a stack to his right. Then he wrote instructions to the custodian of the Archivum Secretum Apostolicum Vaticanum, the Vatican Secret Archives, to place what was being delivered inside his personal storage file, D 217. Without authorization from the pope or secretary of state, no one—not even the wealthiest and most powerful person in the country—would be permitted access to the archives.

When he was finished, he signed the paper and affixed his seal, after which he took another piece of stationery and wrote on it, "Archivum Arcis Armarium D 217." He then signed his name and affixed his seal on this page as well. He kept this authorization at the back of his ledger in the event he was being watched or followed and needed someone to retrieve his insurance policy from the custodian. But he realized that an insurance policy worked only if both sides knew what was at stake. Therefore, he sent a note outlining what he'd done to Duke Rizzo. He hoped this would provide the leverage he needed to get his business partner to buy back his investment portfolio. Unfortunately, he couldn't have been more wrong.

Duke Federigo Rizzo read the letter he had received from Casaroli and placed it within his diary, a book in which he recorded his business dealings as well as his personal opinions. The patriarch often thought that what he was accumulating was one long confession of every crime in which he'd participated—from theft to the murder of a pope. But the narcissistic founder of the Bank of Rizzo believed it important that future generations know what it had taken to create the empire he would give them and what they must be prepared to do to maintain the Rizzo family fortune. He kept what he'd written in a dual-level secure room, hidden behind a false wall in his study within the mansion he'd recently built, with everyone involved in its construction now at the bottom of an Italian lake as a result of a terrible boating accident.

The patriarch wasn't intimidated by Casaroli's threat of exposure. On the contrary, he considered the threat impotent and, in a way, a relief. Rizzo reasoned that if the ledgers and the cardinal's confession were in the Vatican Secret Archives, then only Casaroli and the pope could access them. And given that there were miles of books and documents within that space, it was improbable that even future popes would happen upon what Casaroli had hidden, meaning that the information would eventually be lost to history.

Rizzo finished his diary entry and returned the book to its shelf within the hidden room. He then summoned his chief problem solver to terminate his partnership with Cardinal Ettore Casaroli.

The acting bishop of Rome was walking back from the Sistine Chapel, where along with eight Swiss Guards and high-ranking members of the Curia, he had just escorted the embalmed body of Clement. Tomorrow he would transfer the former pope's body to the Chapel of the Blessed Sacrament in St. Peter's Basilica, where Clement would lie in state for three days. At the end of that time, Clement would be brought to the Chapel of the Canons and put inside a wooden casket, which would be placed into a lead casket, which in turn would be put into a burnished pine casket. Once this process was complete, the triple casket would be taken to St. Peter's and placed in a crypt until the pontiff's final tomb was prepared. Casaroli would have loved to put Clement into an empty tomb below St. Peter's, of which there were several, close the lid, and carve Clement's name on the outside. Done. Instead, he was forced to keep the mandatory and time-consuming schedule that the church had laid out for the burial of a pope. Given that coalitions were always fragile and usually held together by the flimsiest of strings, the acting pontiff was a bundle of nerves as he plodded through days of what he considered to be ceremonial nonsense. Casaroli understood that he needed to convene the conclave and elect the agreed-upon cardinal to the throne before any of the other influential cardinals changed their minds. Another delay could force the election of another interim pope—something Casaroli was keen to avoid because the last one had taken ten years to die.

Casaroli decided not to move his office to the papal suites, which were on the third level of the building, even though he was the acting pontiff. Instead, he would retain his small office on the ground floor because in his deplorable physical condition, there was no way he would be able to perform his duties if he had to constantly traverse three flights of stairs. He decided to prepare for his next stint as secretary of state. Sitting in his desk chair, which had been especially crafted to accommodate his girth and modified to accept his three-hundred-plus pounds, he turned his attention to putting together a list of those within the Vatican who had been especially loyal to Clement and hesitant to accede to Casaroli's demands. Each needed to be transferred from the Vatican if he was to have an iron grip on the curia.

The cardinal had just picked up a quill and was about to dip it into the inkwell when there was a knock at the door. After Casaroli called for the person to enter, a priest in his midtwenties shyly poked his head inside and asked if he could bring the acting pontiff something to eat and drink. Casaroli had never been known to turn down either and told the priest to bring him a plate of beef and a bottle of wine.

When his meal arrived, he pushed his work aside and poured himself a goblet of wine from Montalcino, his favorite. He drained the contents of the glass and poured himself another before carving his beef. When he had finished both, he pushed his tray aside and went back to what he'd been working on.

Two hours after delivering the cardinal his meal, the young man dressed as a priest reentered Casaroli's office. The secretary of state was slumped forward on his desk, his eyes open and his mouth agape. Rizzo's assassin picked up the tray containing the empty plate and wine bottle and left the office. He would take his time returning to Milan. There was no hurry. Word of the cardinal's death would outpace him, and the patriarch would know long before he arrived that he'd accomplished his task.

CHAPTER 10

DUKE RODOLFO RIZZO'S plan to have Bruno lead him to where his father had hidden the ledgers was derailed when the chief inspector found a piece of the duke's Range Rover's grille on the mountain road. Instead of pursuing the corruption associated with the false bank statements that had been placed in his father's briefcase, a trail that led away from Rizzo, the inspector was now investigating the accident. This was extremely bad news to the patriarch because his research had showed that Mauro Bruno was a legend within the Polizia di Stato who had solved nearly every case in which he was involved. Therefore, he expected Mauro Bruno to eventually discover that his father's car had been pushed off the road by the patriarch's vehicle, and he subsequently would consider Rizzo to be the person who'd orchestrated the mishap. And when Bruno eventually found the ledgers, as Rizzo believed he would, he'd rightly conclude that this was the reason his father had been killed. After that, the natural progression of events would result in his goose not only being cooked but kept over the flame until it was incinerated.

After lighting a cigar and telling one of his men to bring him a double espresso, Rizzo sat back in his deeply cushioned brown leather chair and considered his next step in the game of chess he was playing with Bruno. An hour later, he set the remnant of his cigar on the silver tray beside him, got up from his chair, and walked to the windows overlooking the lake and the town. The answer to his problem, he believed, would be simple to implement. At that moment Rizzo believed that he was about to call checkmate and solve his problem with Bruno and the ledgers in one bold move, when in fact his match with Bruno was just beginning.

Bruno left the Range Rover dealership deep in thought. Given what he'd just been told regarding the ownership of the damaged Range Rover, along with his observations of the tire tracks on the narrow mountain road, he was certain that his father's death had not been an accident. It was therefore time to go to the local police, tell them what he'd discovered, report the ransacking of his father's home, and show them the papers he'd found in his father's briefcase. Calling the Milan office of the Polizia di Stato, he verified that Inspector Elia Donati was assigned to investigate his father's death as well as the string of murders he'd learned about from the coroner.

He drove to the inspector's office, which was in a government building several hundred yards from city hall, and showed his state police identification creds to lobby security. He was then given the location of Donati's office on the fifth floor of the renovated nineteenth-century structure. The large rectangular brown-brick building, which housed several departments within the municipal government, was built around a central courtyard filled with yellow acacia, maple, and ash trees, all of which were bordered by a garden of Boston and English ivy. Since space in Venice was at a premium, plush greenery and gardens were rare, and Bruno envied those who worked in such a garden-like setting.

As he stepped off the elevator, the chief inspector stopped and took in the layout of the floor, its modern interior a stark contrast to what one might expect within a nineteenth-century building. There were two areas with private offices, which weren't so private because the walls between them consisted entirely of glass. One ran along the outside windows and had a city view, whereas those surrounding the square hole in the middle of the floor, since the building was constructed around a central courtyard, overlooked the urban forest below. Cubicles filled the space between the two office areas. Bruno had been told by the officer downstairs that the person he was looking for was in the far-right corner office of this center grouping.

When he arrived at Donati's office, Bruno saw a middle-aged woman seated at a cubicle just outside the door to the inspector's inner office. She was a statuesque woman with flowing black hair, an ample bosom, and shapely legs that looked like they belonged to someone twenty years her junior. She was typing on her keyboard while looking at the large computer screen situated in the center of her desk and seemed not to notice him. Showing his police credentials, Bruno interrupted her and asked to see the inspector. She told him to wait while she went into Donati's office. Thirty seconds later, she returned and informed him that the inspector had an impossibly busy schedule, but as a courtesy, he would be able to see Bruno one week from today.

Bruno wasn't buying it and was openly irritated at what could only be interpreted as a lack of professional courtesy among fellow officers, where "impossibly busy" didn't enter into the equation. He walked past the assistant and entered Donati's office. The statuesque brunette ran after Bruno and gave him an angry stare that a mafia boss would be proud of. Profusely apologizing to Donati for letting him get past her, she motioned for Bruno to leave. He ignored her gestures.

Donati was in his midthirties, stood six feet tall, had black hair that he combed straight back, and used enough mousse to keep every hair in place during a category 4 hurricane. He was tan, clean-shaven, and impeccably dressed in a tan suit, white shirt, and light blue tie. His shoes, from what Bruno could see through the glass desktop, looked as if they'd been polished by a military recruit.

"Who are you?" Donati demanded as he rose from his chair, his arrogance and irritation apparent in the tone and forcefulness of his voice.

"As I informed your assistant, I'm Chief Inspector Mauro Bruno from the Venice section of the Polizia di Stato. I'm told that you're the one assigned to investigate my father's death, as well as other recent murders in the city."

"I'm investigating the deaths you mentioned," Donati acknowledged, sitting back down, "but your father died in a car accident. No investigation is necessary. Now if you'll speak with my assistant, she'll schedule your appointment for one week from today. We can speak then. As you correctly noted, I have a number of murders to investigate, and I don't have time for such interruptions." Donati went back to what he had been doing at his desk.

Bruno, his face red with anger, stepped forward, placed his father's briefcase on the floor beside one of the two padded chairs, and sat down. "Perhaps I wasn't clear. I wasn't asking for an appointment. I was telling you that we are going to meet and discuss several pertinent matters—now." Bruno spoke in a tone that a CEO might use to redress someone further down the hierarchy of management who'd questioned his authority.

Donati's eyes disengaged from the document on his desk, and his head rose.

"We both work for the Polizia di Stato," Bruno continued, crossing his legs, "except you have the rank of inspector, and I am a chief inspector. I may not reside in Milan, but my rank is national and entitles me to certain privileges throughout the country, among which is the right to speak with subordinates as I deem necessary. Perhaps you slept through that lesson at the academy."

Donati's cheek muscles went taut, and he clenched his teeth so hard that it appeared he might break a tooth. At the same time, he tightened his grip on the Montblanc pen he was holding until his knuckles turned white. While this was happening, Bruno maintained eye contact and refused to blink or look away. Several seconds after they locked eyes on one another, Donati apparently realized that this was a battle he couldn't win. He looked away, took a deep breath, and told his assistant, who'd been standing at the back of the room, to leave and hold his calls.

Once they were by themselves, Bruno spoke first. "Now to business. I found these documents in my father's briefcase," he said, removing the five pieces of paper and handing them to Donati. "As you'll see, your late mayor appeared to be in contact with an informant who claimed to have two loose-leaf binders containing documentation, in the form of ledgers, that proved there was massive corruption within the government. As evidence, he enclosed three bank statements, although he redacted the individuals' names and account numbers."

As Bruno spoke, Donati looked at each of the five pieces of paper and thoroughly read each. The inspector's posture gradually became less rigid, indicating that he was beginning to calm down.

"The mayor apparently believed the informant and agreed to his terms," Bruno continued. "In return, the mayor was given the binders, which he eventually hand-delivered to the city's chief prosecutor—my father."

Once Donati had finished reading the papers, he looked up and asked, "Do you know where these binders are?" The arrogance in his voice had lowered a notch.

"Possibly. If I locate them, you'll be the first to know."

"And because of this," Donati said, raising one of the bank statements in front of him, "you believe that your father's car accident was actually a well-planned murder."

"That and two other reasons. First, when I arrived from Venice and went to his home, I saw that it had been ransacked. But nothing of value was taken. That tells me that the intruder was looking for something specific—possibly the two binders that are mentioned in these documents."

"Why didn't you report this?"

"At first, I believed the break-in was unrelated to my father's death. After all, I hadn't seen what you're holding in your hand. Therefore, reporting it wasn't a priority—understanding what had happened on that mountain road and arranging for his entombment were. Once I concluded that his death wasn't an accident"—Bruno held up his hand before Donati could interrupt, indicating that he would explain shortly—"I wanted to see if those who had searched the residence would place me under surveillance. If so, that would tell me they didn't find what they were looking for during the break-in."

"And?"

"The black VW Golf that was parked across the street when I left my father's residence has been following me all day. In fact, it was pulling into a parking space on the street in front of this building as I was coming to see you."

"Wait here," Donati said, getting up from his desk and walking to an outer perimeter office that faced the front of the building. When he returned, he sat down and shook his head. "I didn't see the car you described. But Volkswagen is the second-most popular brand in Milan next to Fiat, so it's possible you did see a vehicle of this type in both locations, only not the same car."

Donati had the quizzical look of someone who was on the fence about whether to believe what he'd been told. Apparently not willing to challenge Bruno, he continued. "You mentioned two reasons for believing that your father's death wasn't an accident. The first was the ransacking, your words, of his residence. What's the second?"

Bruno removed the broken piece of grille from his father's briefcase and handed it to Donati.

"What's this?"

"It's a piece of the front grille of a 2018 Holland & Holland Range Rover, which is currently being repaired at a local dealership. I found it at the exact spot where my father's Fiat went over the cliff. I believe another vehicle pushed my father's car off the road because the Fiat's tire tracks were nearly perpendicular to another wider set of tracks, possibly from this vehicle. I believe that when the two vehicles collided, this piece of grille broke off and became embedded in the brush at the edge of the cliff."

"I'll examine the tire tracks, although there could be a number of explanations, including your father swerving at the last second to avoid the edge."

"That's a possibility," Bruno admitted. "But don't you find it curious that both my father and his deputy died on the same day?"

"Coincidences happen. Did the dealer tell you who owns the Range Rover?" Donati asked, getting back to the subject of the grille.

"Duke Rodolfo Rizzo."

Donati smiled and shook his head. "Quite an accusation based on a broken piece of grille that could be explained any number of ways," Donati said. "But of course, you're the great Mauro Bruno and have infallible skills of deduction. So the most respected banker in Italy decided to kill your father and make his death look like an accident, which is what I believe you're implying, instead of sending a dozen or more seasoned lawyers to disprove an accusation of corruption—that is your infallible conclusion."

Bruno didn't respond. Instead, he leaned back in his chair and put his hands together in a steeple gesture, sensing that the inspector had more to say.

"I'll tell you what I'm willing to do, Chief Inspector. I'll investigate your father's accident as if it was a homicide, because I have nothing but time on my hands. I'll also investigate the circumstances relating to how a portion of the grille from the patriarch's car came to be near the spot where your father went off the mountain road. If you'll give me your cell number, I'll keep you abreast of any developments. May I keep what you've given me?"

Bruno said that he could keep the materials and gave Donati his number.

As Bruno left the building and began walking to his car, he saw a black Volkswagen Golf leaving a parking space halfway down the street. As he ran toward the vehicle, the driver apparently saw Bruno approaching because the VW made a quick U-turn and sped away before he could see the driver's face. So much for Donati's eyesight.

Elia Donati watched Bruno get into the elevator and waited until the doors had closed before he swiveled his desk chair around, so that no one would see him remove the burner phone from his jacket pocket. The call he initiated lasted approximately five minutes, after which he placed what Bruno had given him into his Gucci messenger bag and left his office, telling his assistant that he'd see her in the morning.

CHAPTER 11

THE BLACK TWO-DOOR BMW 528i coupe stood out in an outdoor employee parking lot dominated by motorcycles, bicycles, and a variety of inexpensive cars. Bruno watched as Donati got into the vehicle, which would seem to be financially out of his reach, and exited the lot. The chief inspector suspected that Donati's early departure from the office was highly unusual for him, given his "impossibly busy" schedule. Yet the Venetian detective had expected it because he believed that he'd hit a nerve in saying that he possibly knew the location of the binders his father had been given and in indicating that the grille fragment from the scene of the crash had come from the patriarch's Range Rover. It wasn't a stretch to connect the dots and conclude that Donati would want to discuss the meeting with someone who might have been involved in his father's death.

Bruno followed the BMW out of Milan, and as soon as it got off at the Bellagio exit, he took his foot from the accelerator and increased the distance between the two vehicles. Since he had grown up in Milan and came to Lake Como often, the Venetian detective was familiar with the twisting, narrow two-lane road to which the exit led, and he knew that there was no way to keep the BMW in sight without Donati realizing he was being followed. Bruno let the sportscar speed out of view.

The road that Bruno was on hadn't existed three decades ago. The only way to get to Bellagio then had been an access road that added ten miles to the journey. But according to rumors, Duke Rodolfo Rizzo had decided he'd had enough of the circuitous route that he and his guests had to take to get to his estate and had lobbied the government to build the current exit and a road that led past his residence. Most knew that lobbying and bribery were synonymous in Italy.

Ten minutes after leaving the highway, Bruno passed two massive gates that protected a private road leading to the patriarch's mansion, an enormous structure surrounded by extensive landscaping that dominated the top of a mountain. Bruno passed the estate's entrance without stopping to avoid being scrutinized by the two gatepost cameras. But he did see Donati's car on the road leading to the mansion, which supported his previous conclusion that the patriarch was involved in his father's death.

Since there was nothing more to be gained by sticking around, Bruno decided to go to the funeral home to spend a few moments with his father and check on the arrangements for the entombment. Later, he'd go to the place where he believed the binders were hidden. It was a solid plan, but he would not get to execute the final part of it.

Davide Sartori had been sitting in the Chevy Suburban for hours, ever since the patriarch had given him this task over the objections of the stick man. Rizzo knew that the ex-mafia hitman was a specialist in kidnapping and had given him the job based on that reputation. Now Sartori was waiting outside the funeral home for Bruno to return to his car.

He'd staked out the facility early on because he knew that sooner or later, Bruno would show up to pay his last respects to his father, who was to be entombed the following day. The ex-mafia thug believed that a successful kidnapping was all about patience. He had therefore shown up long before he believed Bruno would arrive and had staked out a position that hid him from scrutiny but at the same time gave him a large field of view. Unfortunately, however, that view wasn't large enough. The chief inspector had parked at the back of the parking lot because, unbeknownst to Sartori, he wanted to have a cigarette or two with some privacy. By the time the hitman-kidnapper saw him, Bruno was entering the funeral home.

Sartori repositioned the Suburban to take in both Bruno's vehicle and the funeral door entrance. After slamming his fist on the dash to let off some steam, he lit a joint and tried to calm down. His original plan had been to grab Bruno as he exited his car and force him at gunpoint into the back of the Suburban, where he had two pair of flex-cuffs ready to secure the chief inspector. His new plan, since Bruno would be walking toward him and would probably be suspicious of anyone waiting in the parking lot of a funeral home, would have to be a bit more creative.

After working through the details of a small chapel service for his father, followed by his entombment within the family mausoleum, Bruno walked out of the funeral home. As a chief inspector he was used to seeing dead bodies, but the emotional strain of viewing the remains of the person who'd raised him was again greater than he'd expected, especially since he now realized that his father's death hadn't been an accident and that someone had robbed him of something irreplaceable. He was angry and physically and mentally exhausted when he got into his car.

Bruno debated whether to go to his father's home and get a good night's sleep or look for the binders in the only place he believed they could be. That debate seesawed before finally tipping in favor of the search, when Bruno realized there was a possibility that his father had died to protect the two binders. Therefore, no matter how tired he was, he would get off his ass and go to what he considered the family's secret safe-deposit box. Most importantly, even though he couldn't detect that he was being watched, he had to assume that he was. That meant taking a wandering route to his family's site to detect and lose his tail. Growing up in the area, he was confident that he could make that happen.

The chief inspector had just fastened his seat belt and started the car when he was hit simultaneously in the face and left side of his head. Having been rendered nearly unconscious, he tried to focus and regain his senses. The blows had happened so quickly that Bruno had no idea what had happened. Stunned, he now saw that his steering wheel and left door airbags had been activated and were now lying limp. His vision and mental acuity were still below the waves but starting to surface when he looked over his left shoulder and thought he saw a large vehicle slowly backing away from his Fiat Grande Punto. As his senses began to normalize, he saw that the driver of the other vehicle, now ten yards away, was getting out of what appeared to be a black Chevy Suburban and was carrying a suppressed handgun in his right hand.

As Bruno scrambled into the passenger seat to try to open the right front door and escape, his head was below the dash, so he didn't see the expensive imported vehicle that began sounding its horn and flashing its headlights as it approached. Nor did he see the Suburban's driver turn and send round after round into that vehicle, or the driver of the imported vehicle responding by holding a handgun outside his window and returning fire. Bruno missed all that as he pushed open the passenger door and tumbled onto the asphalt pavement of the parking lot. He did, however, hear the incessant sounding of the horn, the gunshots, and a squeal of tires. Looking slightly to his left, he saw the Suburban race out of the parking lot and rapidly accelerate away from the funeral home.

A moment later, a steady cadence of footsteps approached. Bruno was too exhausted to stand and see who'd saved his life. Instead, he sat up against his vehicle and waited to see who came into view. It was the last person in the world he expected to see.

CHAPTER 12

T HE BISTRO WHERE the two men sat was less than ten minutes from the funeral home. Earlier, Bruno's Fiat had been placed on a flatbed and hauled away. And although Donati's previously pristine BMW was still drivable, it had a shattered front window, several bullet holes in its leather seats—two of them directly where his head would have been had he not ducked—and several other holes in the hood. Donati had already requested that all units in the area be on the lookout for a black Suburban, but he had realized even as he made the call that it was an exercise in futility because the Suburban, which was easily recognizable in a city of compact and mini cars, would soon be torched or destroyed in some other manner.

"Mind if I ask you a question?" Bruno said once the server had delivered their espressos and walked out of earshot.

Donati shrugged, indicating he didn't have an issue.

"The car, the suit, your briefcase," Bruno said, pointing to the Gucci messenger bag beside Donati. "How do you afford it?"

Donati's smile indicated that this wasn't the first time he'd been asked this question. "My father is an executive at Kering, which owns Gucci and a number of other luxury brands. I shop off the rack, so to speak, whenever I like. My family is also quite wealthy, which gives me the opportunity to do what I want with my life. The BMW, by the way, is in my father's name."

Donati had gotten rid of his attitude toward Bruno. Whether that was because both men could have lost their lives moments earlier or because he now believed what Bruno had told him was unclear. The subsequent conversation between them seemed to be between two men on equal footing and on their way to becoming friends.

"Why a police officer? Even with your inspector ranking, a waiter at one of Milan's finer restaurants makes more money than either you or I. Surely your father has enough influence to get you a better-paying job."

"Let me tell you a story," Donati said, leaning back in his chair. He looked past Bruno's shoulder, seemingly at nothing. "As a youth, I was shy and introverted and didn't have many friends. My parents spoiled me, and I got anything I wanted. Therefore, I was shielded from the brutality of the real world." Donati then told Bruno personal details of his tough, rich life—being beaten up for coming to school in a limo, which led him to the school infirmary four times, bullies wanting his cash, and so on. Soon enough, Donati told Bruno, he realized that the bullies' extortion would stop only if they feared him. And this part he said with a slight smirk on his face. He got into shape and learned martial arts, and soon the shoe was on the other foot. When those bullies met the new young Donati, they became afraid. And when they shifted their focus from young Donati to the weakest of those at the school whose parents had money, he decided to be a hero. He became the others' protector and found he liked helping those who couldn't help themselves. That was what did it. After college, he had joined the Polizia di Stato.

Bruno was impressed with what he'd heard, but he still didn't know if it was a practiced story intended to gain someone's trust or the unvarnished truth. He still had several questions he needed answered before he would believe Donati.

"It's quite a coincidence that you happened along when you did."

"It wasn't a coincidence. I had you followed. After you left, I called my lead investigator, who has an office just off the ground-floor lobby and told him you were coming down the elevator and to follow you. Apparently, you didn't trust me any more than I blindly believed the story you told me, because he said that you waited by the employee parking lot and followed me to Duke Rizzo's estate. He also said that you were being followed by one of the duke's men, who was driving a black VW Golf—the same car you mentioned in my office. That made me curious as to why you were being followed."

"As long as we're addressing curiosity, why did you go to Duke Rizzo's estate immediately after our meeting? A suspicious person might conclude that you wanted to discuss my visit and share the information I'd left with you."

"I did, in fact, show him everything that you left with me. You should also know that I called him on the burner phone that I always keep on me," Donati said, taking the phone from his pocket and laying it on the table, "rather than using my personal cell."

"Why?"

"I use the burner phone because I don't want my cellular number associated with the duke. He's always being investigated, and a request for his phone records would show me as one of the people who has had contact with him. The government might get the wrong impression and assume we have a business relationship."

"Do you?"

"The duke has always tried to recruit me, which is why he takes my calls. It's a dance we do. I seem to come closer to the dark side by sharing information with him, while he tempts me to join him by providing information beyond my reach. On various occasions, that has allowed me to arrest criminals who've been operating below my radar. I have no doubt that in providing such information, the duke was ridding himself of competition. Nevertheless, the information he has given me has resulted in the conviction of nearly a dozen really bad people. In this situation, I showed him the five pieces of paper you left with me along with the piece of grille, which apparently came from his Range Rover."

"Was he surprised?"

"Not at all. He said that one of his men had an accident and acknowledged that the grille fragment belonged to his vehicle. He also said that he'd never seen the statements or letters before."

"So what did you accomplish by going there?"

"I maintained the link between us. Also, I saw the person who slammed into your car with the Chevy Suburban. It was Davide Sartori, an ex-mafia assassin who's in the duke's employ. I know this because I've seen him before at the duke's estate and ran a background search on him previously."

"Then you can issue a warrant for his arrest."

"A waste of time. Any good lawyer could get Sartori off because the patriarch and every one of his employees will vouch that he was at the estate the entire time. And by the way, the duke has a multitude of very competent attorneys on retainer. I know because I've spoken to many of them during past investigations. So did your father, I believe. In addition, we won't get any prints off the vehicle Sartori used, which I'm certain belonged to the patriarch, because it'll have been destroyed by now."

"Expensive."

"Rizzo can afford it."

"Anything else you'd like to share?" Bruno asked facetiously.

"That the duke somehow managed to place the papers you showed me inside your father's briefcase."

"How?"

"Because I saw Luciano Gismondi, the duke's chief assassin, turn his head toward the duke when I removed the papers from my briefcase, even though I hadn't mentioned what they were. Obviously, he'd already seen them. Second, the duke quickly shook his dead at Gismondi when he saw the papers, seemingly telling him to keep it under control. And third, when I arrived at the duke's office, I asked him for a piece of paper so that I could take notes. He obliged. If you look at the five pieces of paper in your father's briefcase and the one that Rizzo gave me, you'll see they're the same—an expensive linen blend. Almost everyone uses cotton blend, which is cheaper. The odds are almost nonexistent that these three anomalies are coincidences."

Donati removed the sheet that Rizzo had given him from his messenger bag, along with the pieces of paper that Bruno had left, and placed them side by side on the table. "This is not your typical 75 GSM copy paper. This is 151 GSM or higher linen paper, which is triple the price."

"GSM?"

"Grams per square meter. The weight of the paper."

Bruno picked up the linen sheet that Donati had received from Rizzo, along with one of the pages he'd left with the inspector, and looked at both closely before placing them back on the table. "You're a paper expert?"

"My parents use linen paper. Over the years I've bought it online for them more times than I can count. It's what wealthy families use to impress one another."

"All right. So Sartori slammed his vehicle into mine, and the airbags went off. I was spaced out, but I could still see him walking toward me with a gun in his hand. Why didn't he put a double tap in my skull?"

"The only explanation is that the duke told him not to kill you. Otherwise, an ex-mafioso like Sartori wouldn't think twice about murdering you. I believe that he was going to kidnap you so that the duke could ask, probably not all that gently, where your father hid the two binders. And once you provided that information, you would have been killed."

"If the binders don't contain bank statements, then what's in them?"

"Something that must be critically important to Rizzo. Also, I think it's important to note that the informant called them ledgers rather than binders, which implies financial statements," Donati said.

"As good an assumption as any," Bruno replied.

Bruno had to admit that what he was hearing made sense. Still, there were a few blank spaces that needed to be filled in. "How did you, and not your investigator who was following me, happen to be at the funeral home? Your timing was perfect in leaving the estate in time to come to my rescue."

"My investigator followed you to the funeral home and knew you'd be there for a while. He sent me a text asking if I wanted him to wait. Since I wasn't getting anything more from the duke, I texted him to head home. I then decided to go to the funeral home myself to tell you about my conversation with Rizzo."

Bruno downed what remained of his espresso and moved his empty cup to the side. "I believe it's time we work together, get the binders containing the ledgers, and see what the duke is willing to kill so many people to obtain."

"Do you know where they are?" Donati asked.

"We'll both find out when we get there."

CHAPTER 13

"TAKE THE SUBURBAN into the mountains and push it into one of the ravines," Rizzo said to Gismondi as soon as Sartori returned. "Make sure you're high enough so that the car is heavily damaged, Luciano."

Gismondi nodded his acceptance of the order.

"Where's Mauro Bruno at this moment?"

"After Sartori's call," Gismondi said, giving his nemesis a look that said he despised his failure, "one of my men took over surveillance and followed Bruno and Inspector Donati to a bistro not far from the funeral home."

The patriarch turned to Sartori, who was quietly seated to his left. The ex-mafioso was fidgeting in his chair, much like a schoolchild sitting in front of the principal for a major misdeed.

"Listen to me carefully, Davide. There can be no mistakes this time," Rizzo said in a menacing tone that made it apparent that failure would have the most dire consequences. "Kidnap both Bruno and Donati and bring them here. If either knows the location of the ledgers, I'll find out. If they don't, you'll kill them and send their bodies to the bottom of the lake. Take whomever you need with you, but get this done today."

Having received his orders, Sartori silently got up and called on one of the duke's bodyguards, Antonio Rossi, who was an all-around badass but had a brain the size of a walnut, to accompany him. They took the elevator down to the garage, where Sartori selected a G65 AMG Mercedes SUV, a $220,000 tank, while Rossi went to get his personal vehicle from the adjoining underground space.

After Sartori and Gismondi had left, Rizzo went into the vault adjoining his study and began to document and analyze what had occurred in the past day. Like every other patriarch before him, he was candid when making his diary entries so that future generations could not only have a record of his accomplishments but also learn from his mistakes.

He previously had written that getting the ledgers back was important because they exposed substantive misdeeds by the family's first patriarch—Duke Federigo Rizzo. If the content of the ledgers became known, the resulting shit storm, although he used more eloquent words, would damage the family's financial foundation, the Bank of Rizzo, and evaporate the stock price. He also had written about his concern over the single page containing the words "Archivum Arcis Armarium D 217" because it exposed the family's deepest and darkest secret, which was far more serious than generational financial thievery. Rizzo's hand had shaken slightly as he made this notation.

In his latest entry he noted that in retrospect he should have just put a bullet into Salvatore Bruno and forgotten about the accident scenario. There would have been an intense investigation by the state police, probably including Mauro Bruno. But so what? He would have weathered that storm, the same as he had the many others that had confronted him over the years. He went on to write that he'd compounded that mistake by ordering Sartori to kidnap Mauro Bruno, a plan that had fallen apart when Donati somehow came to the rescue. He would have to determine how that had occurred. Nevertheless, the result was that both inspectors probably suspected that he was behind the death of Salvatore Bruno and the attempted kidnapping of his son.

After finishing the entry, Rizzo placed his diary back in the vault and ordered one of the guards to accompany him into the basement, where he needed to prepare for the arrival of the two guests that Sartori would be bringing shortly.

Donati noticed that they were being followed not long after he and Bruno left the bistro. The gray Lancia Ypsilon remained a steady hundred yards behind the BMW, even as Donati weaved in and out of light traffic to determine if he indeed had a tail or was being paranoid. Halfway to their destination, he saw the Lancia get off the highway. But it was quickly replaced by a G65, a vehicle he was familiar with because his father had once looked at buying such a car. The Mercedes similarly kept its distance, despite his weaving through traffic and varying his speed.

"The Lancia is gone, and a Mercedes SUV has taken its place," Donati said to Bruno, who was in the passenger seat. "We're ten minutes away from the destination you gave me. What do you want to do?"

"Can you lose him?"

"No. The next turnoff is ours, and after that, a single road takes us to our destination."

"Let's put off retrieving the ledgers until after my father's entombment tomorrow. It'll be easy to get them then, assuming they're where I believe they are."

"In that case, I'll drop you off at your father's house."

Donati intentionally passed the exit that Bruno earlier had told him to take and instead took the next highway off-ramp and followed Bruno's directions to his father's residence.

"It looks like the Mercedes wagon gave up, or maybe it was never following us in the first place. Being a police officer has made me eternally paranoid," Donati confided.

"It's better to be paranoid than dead."

Donati smiled. "Did you bring a weapon with you from Venice?"

"I didn't think I'd need it."

"Then take mine," Donati said, removing his shoulder holster and handing it to Bruno. "I have another at home."

Bruno looked at the Beretta 92FS, admiring it as he took it from Donati. "The department didn't buy this, did they?"

"If your life is important, you don't settle for second best. This nine-millimeter is the most accurate that Beretta makes and can be used at distances greater than fifty yards. You'll also need these." Donati took two extra clips from the glove compartment and handed them to Bruno.

The chief inspector put both clips in his jacket pocket. He told Donati that he'd see him in the morning and, holding the Beretta in his right hand, walked toward the residence.

Sartori and Rossi watched from the bushes as Donati handed over his weapon and clips. Both had arrived at the residence a minute ahead of Donati and Bruno, having raced down side streets at speeds substantially faster than Donati's impaired BMW was doing on residential streets. Sartori, who'd gotten off an exit earlier than the inspectors and Rossi, had rolled the dice, believing that Bruno was headed for his father's home. If he wasn't, then that error in judgment was not something that he'd ever relay to the duke—not if he wanted to live.

Donati was watching Bruno approach the front door of the residence when Rossi silently approached and put his left fist through the side window of the BMW. Sartori, who was standing to his left, then pressed the trigger on his Taser and sent the wires through the shattered opening. In a split second, 1,200 volts hit Donati's body. The inspector pulsated a bit in his seat, immediately forfeiting voluntary control of his muscles. He went rigid, and his brain lost all ability to process new information. Rossi then opened the door, and he and Sartori dragged the inspector out of the car and across the street. They were just about to the trees when they heard someone order them to stop and raise their hands.

Rossi was the first to respond, turning and pointing his gun in the direction of the voice. That was a mistake. The impact from the Beretta's 9mm projectile that hit his chest hurled him backward and onto the ground before he even had a chance to aim. While this was happening, Sartori let go of Donati and drew his gun, managing to fire several times in Bruno's direction. But because there were no lights behind the detective and Sartori therefore couldn't see him, all the assassin's shots went wide. While Bruno was lucky in not being an easy target, Sartori wasn't. He was standing near the row of streetlamps edging the park, which made him a well-exposed target. Bruno's single return shot found the center of his forehead.

Bruno ran to Donati and knelt beside him. He took off his own jacket, folded it, and placed it under the inspector's head to act as a cushion. Over the course of the next ten minutes, the inspector became more cognizant of his surroundings and began to regain muscle control.

"What happened?" were the first words out of Donati's mouth when he was finally able to speak.

"Two men tried to kidnap you. Fortunately, I had trouble finding the key to the front door in my pants pocket, and it took me a while to finally remember that I'd put it in the side flap of my jacket. When I heard breaking glass coming from the street, I looked toward your car and saw them dragging you out of it. I called for them to stop, and when one of them pointed his gun at me, I fired. The other fired off several rounds, but thankfully, he couldn't get a good bead on me. The same couldn't be said for my shot, and I dropped him."

"Any idea who they might be?" Donati asked.

"One is the person who rammed the Suburban into me. I don't know the other. But it looks like you'll have two more killings to investigate," Bruno said with a smile.

CHAPTER 14

THE CADILLAC FROM the funeral home picked up Mauro Bruno at the villa at 10:00 a.m. to take him to the Cimitero Monumentale, where the funeral director had arranged for a viewing of the casket in the main chapel of the cemetery, along with a eulogy, prior to his father's entombment. Bruno didn't know how many of his father's friends and acquaintances would come because he hadn't sent out announcements, but the funeral director had told him that his father had many friends, quite a few of whom had called and inquired about the service. Therefore, he expected some of them would be in attendance.

The Bruno family mausoleum was a gray granite structure that one entered through an ornate brass doorway. It was in the Catholic section of the cemetery, which was within walking distance of the chapel. The mausoleum had been commissioned by Salvatore Bruno's great-grandfather, a merchant of some standing who had made his fortune by importing silk from the Orient. The interior was constructed of the same granite as the exterior. As one entered, the wall to the left had spaces for twelve caskets, four across and three high. There were also niches for twenty-four cremation urns, six across and four high, within the right wall. A bronze plaque giving the decedent's name, along with the dates of their birth and death, was affixed to each occupied space. A thick granite bench rested against the far wall.

When the Cadillac entered the cemetery, it went directly to the Famedio, a massive white neo-medieval-style building within which the chapel was located. The driver, a slight man in a black livery uniform, parked in front of the main entrance and raced around the vehicle to open Bruno's door. He then waited beside the vehicle as the chief inspector walked into the building.

As Bruno walked into the chapel, he was ill prepared for the two hundred or so people who filled both every available seat in the pews and the standing room within. It was hard to keep the tears from flowing as he walked down the central aisle to a reserved seat in the first row, in front of which his father's casket rested on a raised platform.

After several of his father's friends, at the encouragement of the priest conducting the service, came up to the podium to give their impromptu remembrances, it was Bruno's turn to speak about the person he'd loved and admired. The eulogy gave those in attendance an insight into his father that could only come from a family member. For example, Bruno told the story of the time his father had taught him how to drive. Not being the best student, Bruno put several dents in the family car. His father, believing that people should be given credit for their accomplishments, painted the name "Mauro" over each of the dents so that everyone would know where they had come from. But the fact was that his father wasn't a perfect driver either. Subsequently, when his father left for work one morning, he noticed "Salvatore" painted over two dents that he'd put in the bumper. His father laughed so hard that he could barely breathe. As Mauro grew older, he said, and understood more about life, he had been determined to model himself after his father. This didn't mean becoming an attorney, because he found the profession boring, but meant trying to duplicate his father's integrity, honesty, and decency. This was why, he said, he had become a police officer. Bruno then went on to tell a few stories illustrating his father's strength of character. In the end, there wasn't a dry eye to be found in the chapel, Bruno's included.

Once the service was complete, a procession ensued to the family mausoleum. The pallbearers, young police officers who had admired the crusty chief prosecutor, carried the casket inside, followed by Bruno and the priest. The crypt where the casket was placed was one row from the bottom and the second from the left of the four crypts in that row. Directly to its left was the casket of Mauro Bruno's mother, who'd been entombed ten years earlier. Below were the caskets of Salvatore Bruno's grandfather and father, along with their wives. Once the casket was in its final resting place, the granite door was closed and locked. The priest then excused himself to give Bruno time alone.

The chief inspector knelt before his father's crypt, said a prayer, and then stood and looked at the room's interior. He'd come here every year with his father on their mother and wife's birthday, to remember both her and Salvatore's family. Momentarily setting aside his sorrow, Bruno went to the bench that rested against the far wall, reached underneath, and released a latch. He then lifted the top, which was hinged at either end, and exposed the bench's hollow interior. Inside were two rafts of papers, each bound at the top and bottom with stiff pieces of black leather and tightly secured with a string. On top of one of the stacks was a folded piece of vellum. Bruno didn't see any binders and therefore theorized that the stiff pieces of leather holding the pages of the ledger together were what someone had earlier referred to as a binder, and the term had stuck.

Bruno first unfolded the vellum and saw an emblem at the top that matched the imprint of the red wax seal at the bottom. In between were the handwritten words "Archivum Arcis Armarium D 217," and directly below that was the signature of Cardinal Ettore Casaroli. Not familiar with either the signatory or the Latin words, Bruno put the vellum page in his jacket pocket and untied the string and leather strips around the two stacks of papers. From what he could see, they were both centuries-old accounting ledgers—a long way from the bank statements and explanatory letter that he'd found in his father's briefcase. Needing far more time to determine the significance of what he was holding, he retied the papers and carried them outside. He and Donati could examine them that evening.

As he closed and locked the mausoleum door, he saw that everyone except for his driver and Donati had left. Donati was standing a few yards from the mausoleum, and the driver had just stepped out of the car.

"I see you found them," Donati said, looking at what Bruno was carrying.

"I found something. But one thing is for sure—they're not bank statements."

Donati seemed about to ask exactly what he meant when the driver approached him from behind, removed a gun from a previously hidden shoulder holster, and hit Donati on the back of the head. The man then pointed the gun at Bruno and told him to place both binders in the back seat of the Cadillac, the rear door of which was open.

The chief inspector did as he was told.

"Give my regards to your father when you see him," the man said, leveling his gun at Bruno. "He was a pathetic driver and easy to manipulate. It was child's play running him off the road."

Bruno was starting to reach for his own gun, despite realizing that it probably wouldn't make any difference at this point, when he heard a gunshot. Looking at his chest where the man had pointed his gun, he couldn't see even a trace of blood. But the same couldn't be said about the person who had been holding a gun on him a moment earlier. He seemed to be bleeding badly as he jumped into the Cadillac and accelerated away, the driver's door slamming shut as turned the corner and floored it toward the cemetery exit.

Looking to where Donati had fallen, Bruno saw that he was lying flat on his back and holding a gun. "Are you all right?" Bruno asked, helping him to his feet as people in the cemetery started running toward them.

"Not remotely. This is the second set of Brioni pants that I've ripped in the last twenty-four hours. I really want to kill that son of a bitch."

Bruno had to laugh at the absurdity of Donati's response given what had just happened. "Any idea who that was?" Bruno asked.

"Luciano Gismondi. I've seen him several times at the duke's estate. I didn't notice that he was your driver because I was already inside the chapel when you arrived, and he waited inside the car when you were inside the mausoleum. I blew it when I was looking at you and not him when you walked outside, but I couldn't take my eyes off the papers you were carrying. Sorry."

"You saved my life. Believe me, no apology is necessary."

"Your father picked a very clever hiding place. It's too bad we lost what he was safeguarding."

"Everything except this," Bruno said, taking the folded vellum sheet out of his pocket.

Donati looked at it but had no better understanding of what it meant than Bruno.

"Let's talk to the funeral home director and see what he knows," said Bruno.

"It's as good a place as any to start. My car is over there," Donati said, pointing.

Bruno looked but didn't see it.

"It's the Mercedes G65. My men found it parked a block away from your residence and impounded it, along with a gray Lancia. Since my BMW was towed to the dealer this morning, and the lab is finished taking fingerprints and such from the Mercedes, I decided to appropriate it. I know you won't be surprised if I tell you that it belongs to Duke Rodolfo Rizzo. I thought I'd have another chat with him after we visit the funeral home. It should be interesting driving up in his car. Care to join me?"

Generously speaking, the G65 wasn't the most comfortable of rides, and by the time they reached the funeral home, Bruno was urging Donati to return to the dealer and get his BMW back, missing driver's window and assorted bullet holes notwithstanding.

As expected, the owner of the funeral home had no idea, given the description that Donati provided, who had been driving his company's vehicle or how Gismondi had learned the details of the funeral and what time to show up at Bruno's residence. If Bruno and Donati had to make a guess, it was that the real driver gave Gismondi all the information he needed to pull off this ruse and that he was no longer alive.

While Donati and Bruno were speaking with the funeral home owner, several police officers searched the building and surrounding area. It wasn't long before one of them returned and said that he'd found the driver's body inside a dumpster. After that, a forensics team, the medical examiner, and others began to arrive at the crime scene. By then, Bruno and Donati were in the G65 and on their way to Bellagio.

CHAPTER 15

A S DONATI PULLED the G65 in front of the estate's security gates, the two massive wrought iron structures opened. Donati and Bruno agreed as they entered the estate grounds that the security guard, not being able to see through the car's darkened windows and knowing that the Mercedes belonged to the duke, must have opened the gates on the assumption that someone on the duke's staff was driving.

Pulling in front of the mansion, they got out of the vehicle and headed toward the front door. As they did, Bruno noticed an uneven trail of blood on the gravel driveway indicating that Gismondi had come here directly from the cemetery. He'd just pointed out the blood droppings to Donati when one of the security staff opened the front door and said that the duke was waiting for them in his office. Apparently, their presence had become known as soon as they stepped out of the vehicle, at which point they'd been picked up by a security camera.

Once they were off the driveway and onto the concrete strip leading to the front door, Bruno didn't see any evidence of blood. So whoever had cleaned up after Gismondi had obviously overlooked the driveway.

As they walked into Rizzo's office, Bruno saw huge flames consuming what looked to be paper tinder within the fireplace. Looking closer, he saw the remains of a vellum page disintegrating to ash.

"I hope you don't mind the fire, gentlemen," Rizzo said. "I found it chilly and asked one of my men to locate some tinder. Fortunately, they were able to find some old papers, which worked quite well." The look on Rizzo's face was one of arrogance and invincibility. "Please have a seat," he said, pointing to the two leather chairs in front of his desk.

"Let me first express my condolences for the death of your father," Rizzo continued, in a tone that seemed mechanical rather than heartfelt. "It's a shame someone with his skills died so needlessly in a car accident."

"I'm not sure it was an accident. The chief prosecutor may have been murdered," Donati interjected.

"You believe he was killed?"

Donati said that he was exploring the possibility that the chief prosecutor's car had been pushed off the narrow mountain road. The strident tone in his voice and the stern look on his face indicated that he believed Rizzo to be responsible.

"I had no idea that your father had such enemies," Rizzo said, looking at Bruno. "But I suppose, given what he may have been investigating, that it's not unexpected that he'd have a powerful adversary."

"A cowardly one who was obviously afraid to match intellects with my father in court," Bruno said. "You own a great many luxury vehicles, don't you?"

"One of my many vices, I'm afraid. Although lately," Rizzo said, apparently knowing where Bruno was headed, "several have been stolen. I reported this to the local police and filed a report."

"Credit the thieves with ingenuity," Bruno replied. "To steal your vehicles, they had to get onto your estate, get past armed guards and security cameras, steal the cars from your garage, open the front gates, and drive away without being noticed. If you want my professional opinion, it sounds like an inside job."

Rizzo gave a disapproving look in response to the obvious inference, even though everyone present knew that nothing could leave the estate unless Rizzo gave his permission.

"My security has been inexplicably lax. Is there something else you want to discuss, or did you just come to return my vehicle?" Rizzo's voice and body language said, *You're wasting my time—get out.*

"Unfortunately, your Mercedes is evidence in the murder of two men, Davide Sartori and Antonio Rossi, who were killed while trying to kidnap me," Donati replied. "We'll have to keep it a while longer. Do you know these men?"

"I don't."

"Odd, since they're both on your payroll."

"I don't handle the staff. Someone takes care of that for me."

"How about Luciano Gismondi?"

"Again, I'm not on familiar terms with those I employ. They're servants, nothing more. People who have menial jobs or work every day to make a living are best left to associate with their own kind. Don't you agree?"

The hard stare that Bruno gave Rizzo could only be interpreted as an invitation to stuff that remark where the sun didn't shine, but he refrained from commenting. The reason for this self-control was that his father had told him, following his past verbal exchanges with the duke, that angry outbursts were exactly what Rizzo wanted and that it gave him a great deal of satisfaction to know that the person he'd made angry was powerless against him.

"Good manners dictate that I don't agree or disagree," Bruno responded.

"Then I believe we're done," Rizzo said.

After they rose from their chairs, Donati followed Rizzo to the door, while Bruno diverted to the fireplace.

"I see that your tinder has ignited the logs beneath it. Vellum is always the best tinder," Bruno said, removing the folded vellum page from his jacket pocket and unfolding it so that Rizzo could see the red wax seal. "Perhaps there will be more old papers, as you called them, in the Archivum Arcis Armarium D 217." Bruno knew this was a Hail Mary pass at best.

Rizzo didn't immediately respond, but Bruno knew he'd hit a nerve when the expression on the duke's face transformed from arrogance to outright malevolence.

"Tinder is tricky, Chief Inspector. If one is not careful, it can consume and kill the holder. You should keep that in mind."

Bruno and Donati returned to Milan and went straight to Donati's office, where the chief inspector still seemed to be on the persona non grata list with Donati's attractive assistant, judging from the look he received. Bruno looked over the inspector's shoulder as Donati performed an internet search on Cardinal Ettore Casaroli. They learned that Casaroli had been the papal secretary of state for both Benedict XIII and Clement XII. Donati then typed "Archivum Arcis Armarium D 217" in the search box and hit enter. What appeared on the screen came as a total surprise. D 217 referred to the location of the Chinon Parchment within the Vatican Secret Archives, access to which was given only to the pope, his secretary of state, archive staff, and on rare occasions, scholars.

"According to this Google search," Donati said, "the Chinon Parchment was misfiled and eventually found in September 2001 by Barbara Frale. At the time she was an Italian paleographer at the Vatican Secret Archives. The parchment dates from 1308 and was issued by Pope Clement V to absolve the Knights Templar from charges brought against them by the Inquisition, at least according to most scholars' interpretation."

"I'm not sure the duke is interested in the Knights Templar," Bruno said. "Nor do I believe that Cardinal Casaroli was. It's possible, however, that Casaroli used D 217 as a hiding place within the archives and intentionally misfiled the parchment, which at that point hadn't been looked at in four and a half centuries. Further, he had access to the Vatican Secret Archives. Using that space was as good as having whatever he stored there in a safe-deposit box."

"Casaroli must have had something on the Rizzo family," said Donati, "because the paper in your pocket triggered Rizzo's hot button. Whatever's hidden there must be explosive enough to warrant the death of anyone who knows about it, even three centuries late—the ancestral skeleton in the closet."

"Exactly. It's too bad we lost those two stacks of paper—they might have given us a clue. But you know that he's going to come after this piece of paper," Bruno said, touching his left inside jacket pocket.

"We're in agreement on that. The question is, how do we get into the Vatican Secret Archives, which is technically the pope's personal property and requires his permission for entrance?"

"The way anyone does—through the front door," Bruno responded, with a look of mischief in his eyes.

The Order of Saint Benedict was not a single religious organization because each monastery operated autonomously. Although the abbot primate, the senior monk, was elected by all to that office, his primary function was to represent the various orders at international gatherings and to act as a liaison to the Vatican. Bruno and the current abbot primate had met when the American monk came to Venice and reported that a pickpocket had taken his wallet as he walked through the Piazza San Marco. Bruno had reviewed the recordings of various cameras in the area, spotted the abbot's wallet being lifted, and traced the thief to where he lived. The abbot primate, grateful for the recovery, had told Bruno to call if he needed anything in the future. Today Bruno was going to call in that marker.

Bruno had one of the other inspectors in the Venice office go through his card file to retrieve the abbot primate's number. When they connected, the American remembered not only who Bruno was but also the promise he'd made. After listening to what the chief inspector had to say, he voiced his belief that the Holy Father would decline his request but nevertheless said he would make the call and do his best to get Bruno access.

When the abbot primate got back to Bruno, it was nearly ten in the evening, and their call was brief. After the call ended, Bruno turned to Donati, who was sitting behind his desk, writing a report the size of a novel on what had occurred since the chief inspector first came to his office. Donati had stopped to listen to Bruno's side of the conversation, but this hadn't given him much insight. It wasn't until Bruno smiled that Donati knew the abbot primate had been successful, a fact confirmed when Bruno said, "We're going to Rome."

Gismondi was playing catchup. He'd been told to kill Bruno and Donati, something he looked forward to. But he couldn't find them. He'd gone to Donati's residence and waited for his arrival, expecting that the Milanese police officer would drop Bruno off at his late father's residence and then return home. But after waiting four and a half hours, he threw in the towel and went to Salvatore Bruno's residence. Accessing the security cameras from his cell phone, he saw that no one was at this residence either. It was 10:30 p.m., and he'd gotten nowhere. He called the patriarch and told him that wherever Bruno and Donati were, it wasn't at either of their residences. Since it was late, and Bruno was known to be an early riser, Gismondi said that he believed they were staying somewhere else for the night.

Rizzo listened without comment, then told Gismondi to stay where he was and that he'd get back to him. Playing a hunch, Rizzo went to his computer and looked up flights from Milan to Rome on a travel website. He began calling the various airlines, giving his name as Mauro Bruno and asking them to confirm his flight for that evening. After twenty minutes of calling, he found that Bruno was departing from Linate Airport to Rome's Ciampino airport, which was close to the Vatican. Expedia showed that there was an earlier flight to Rome, but it departed from Milan's larger airport at Malpensa. If Gismondi could make that flight, he would arrive before the inspectors.

Gismondi raced to Malpensa, arriving twenty minutes prior to departure. He left his weapon in his vehicle and bought a ticket at the airline kiosk. Since he'd bought a first-class ticket, he entered the expedited security line and was through the scanner in less than a minute. He ran to his gate at the end of the terminal and was the last to board. If his plane arrived on time, he'd be at the Ciampino airport forty minutes prior to Bruno and Donati's arrival. That would give him enough time to get a rental car and follow them to their hotel. He'd need a weapon, but that wouldn't be a problem. In the morning he'd call one of the patriarch's mafia contacts to obtain what he needed.

Gismondi indeed arrived early and was waiting in his car when he saw Bruno and Donati exit the arrival terminal and queue for a taxi. He followed them to their hotel and, staying far enough back to avoid being seen, was able to observe which rooms they entered. Since he was unarmed, he got himself a room in a motel less than a mile away. He would get a weapon later that morning and then kill Bruno and Donati.

CHAPTER 16

DONATI AND BRUNO arrived at their hotel in Rome at 2:30 a.m. and six hours later took a taxi to the Porta di Santa Anna gate, the technical border crossing between Italy and Vatican City. There they met Marco Cattaneo, the prefect of the Vatican Secret Archives. The head of the pope's personal library was five feet, seven inches tall, and appeared to be in his early fifties. His short black hair was neatly parted to his right, and he tilted the scale at the lighter end of thin. He wore a three-piece charcoal-gray suit, which looked baggy on his slight frame, a white shirt, and a yellow and blue striped tie that reflected his school affiliation. His shoes were highly polished wing tips, and he wore no rings or other jewelry. The two Vatican Swiss Guards who stood beside him checked Bruno and Donati's identification and relayed their acceptance to the prefect.

"Welcome, gentlemen," Cattaneo said as he stepped forward and shook their hands. "I've never before received a call from the Holy Father late at night, much less to tell me to give two nonacademics immediate access to his library. What you're doing must be extremely important to warrant such attention."

"We're both humbled to have access," Bruno replied.

The prefect apparently liked Bruno's response because he smiled. The three then proceeded through the Cortile del Belvedere to another set of guards, who opened the two enormous brass doors behind them. The group continued into the building, passing several pairs of security guards along the way, and were led to a narrow winding metal staircase, which they ascended single file. At the top both Bruno and Donati stood in awe. Before them were over fifty-three miles of dark wooden shelves containing tens of thousands of books, papers, scrolls, and documents dating back to the early days of the church.

"The content of D 217 is waiting for you in this room," Cattaneo said, directing them ahead and to his left.

When they entered the room, they saw an enormous scroll lying on a white cloth atop a large rectangular table.

"This is the Chinon Parchment," the prefect said. "It was written in 1308 and, by the hand of Pope Clement V, absolves the leadership of the Knights Templar from charges brought against them by the Inquisition. But I'm sure you both know that, or you wouldn't have asked to see it."

"Is this all there was in D 217?" Donati asked.

"Yes. In 1308 the archive space referred to as D 217 was assigned to the Chinon Parchment. But in September 2001 it was discovered that the parchment had been misfiled. That mistake was rectified, and it was returned to its proper location. Nothing else resides in this space."

Bruno and Donati looked at each other with questioning expressions.

"Would it be possible for us to look at D 217 so that we can get a feel as to how documents are stored in the archives?" Bruno asked.

The thinly veiled question seemed to imply that Cattaneo hadn't brought them everything or had overlooked something. Either way, it surprised Cattaneo, judging from his gaping mouth.

The prefect seemed to be mulling over his options, undoubtedly thinking that if he turned them down, they might go back to the pope and request a second visit— something he'd prefer to avoid because it would make him look uncooperative. Working at the Vatican for twenty-five years, fifteen as the prefect of the Vatican archives, had taught him that papal bureaucracy required two ingrained traits: flexibility and a willingness to compromise.

"If you'll follow me," Cattaneo said, and he led Bruno and Donati deeper into the archives.

D 217, as it turned out, was a numbered location on a shelf, now empty because the parchment usually stored there was in a viewing room. While the look on Cattaneo's face was one of vindication, Bruno and Donati wore expressions of disappointment.

"I can't accept," Bruno said to Donati, who was standing to his right and beside Cattaneo, "that Cardinal Casaroli would go to the trouble of writing this location on his personal stationery and then placing his seal on it if there wasn't something here besides the Chinon Parchment."

"Especially since Rizzo's face went white and he all but threatened to kill you when you showed him that vellum page," Donati said. "I agree. There's something we're overlooking."

Cattaneo seemed to be all ears as he listened to this exchange. "You mentioned a vellum page with Cardinal Casaroli's signature on it," the prefect said. "Can I see it?"

Bruno took the page from his jacket pocket and handed it to Cattaneo, who unfolded it and stared at the vellum for a full minute, every now and then holding it up to the light above him. "Where did you get this?" the prefect asked, breaking his silence.

"My father, God rest his soul, was the chief prosecutor for Milan. Not long before his death, he was given two large stacks of vellum papers, along with this page. Unfortunately, the papers were stolen before I could fully examine them, but I managed to save what you're holding." Bruno stepped closer to Cattaneo. "What can you tell us about this page?" he asked, touching the sheet that Cattaneo was holding.

"I can tell you that judging from the discoloration and degradation of the ink, it's made from iron salts and tannic acids derived from vegetables, which was common between the fifth and nineteenth centuries. This gave the ink an acidity level somewhere between a lemon and a cup of coffee. Second, during the time Cardinal Casaroli was secretary of state, the Vatican added crushed eggshells to its ink mixtures to counteract the acid. Since there are no rusty halos in the ink on this paper, or holes from an excess of ferrous ions, I can conclude that the ink used by the person who wrote this probably came from the Vatican at the time Cardinal Casaroli served as secretary of state." The prefect paused for just a moment. "Follow me," he then said, without explanation.

Bruno and Donati were led deeper into the secret archives. As Cattaneo walked, he removed a pair of white gloves from his jacket pocket and put them on. When they arrived at their destination, the prefect grabbed an old leather box from a shelf and carried it to a viewing room a short distance away. Placing the box on the desk, he removed a document and laid it on the table. He then put the paper Bruno had given him beside it.

"This is the signature of Cardinal Ettore Casaroli, along with his wax seal," the prefect said, swinging the arm of a stand-mounted magnifying glass over the documents.

After examining the signatures and wax seals of both pages for nearly fifteen minutes, Cattaneo pushed the magnifying glass away and looked toward Bruno and Donati. "The signature on the page you handed me is definitely that of Cardinal Ettore Casaroli. Regarding the seal, in both your document and the paper here beside it, the seals are cracked from age and have blackened soot marks, something that's difficult but not impossible to duplicate. Each seal is also located in the same spot on the page, and both imprints are not perfectly round—an indication of their authenticity. The wax has stained through, in both your paper and the one I have, which is another measure of authenticity. Last, looking at the secretary of state's crest at the top of each paper, we can see that the debossing was done by the same device. There's an almost imperceptible tell in the upper left corner, where the metal on the device imparting the imprint did not have uniform thickness around its circumference. It would be difficult to mechanically duplicate that minor flaw. I can perform carbon-14 dating, but I don't believe that's necessary. What you've given me was written by Cardinal Casaroli."

"Any idea why he was referencing a fourteenth-century document?"

"I don't believe he was. If I were to hazard a guess, I'd say that he intentionally misfiled the Chinon Parchment, knowing that someday a researcher would want to study it and would instead discover what he put in its place."

"But that's not what happened," Donati said.

"No, it isn't. And because access to these archives is highly restricted, it's improbable that someone stole it. The greater likelihood is that whatever the cardinal was hiding in D 217 wasn't returned to that location after someone viewed it. Instead, it was misfiled. It's not an altogether uncommon occurrence. Centuries ago, there was only candlelight to illuminate the interior, which made it difficult to accurately see numbers. An eight could look like a six, and a zero like a nine, for example."

"So what we're looking for could be in another space close to D 217," Bruno said.

"Possibly. I'm intrigued by this. Let's look."

The prefect placed boxes D 210 through D 219, except for D 217, which was still in the room where they'd looked at it, on a cart and transported them into another viewing room. Cattaneo then meticulously examined the contents of each box. He found what they were looking for in D 218. Inside were two bound stacks of vellum along with two individual sheets of paper. Cattaneo picked up one of the individual sheets and began to read. It didn't take long for his eyes to widen in astonishment and his face to lose its color. Without explanation, he summoned the Swiss Guards to immediately escort Bruno and Donati from the archives.

"What just happened?" Donati asked as the two Swiss Guards closed the large brass doors behind them.

"Cattaneo read something on one or both of those papers that he didn't want to share with us. Whatever it was seemed to put the fear of God, pardon the expression, in him. Two seconds later, he threw us out."

"There's nothing we can do about it. The Vatican is a sovereign state and isn't subject to Italian law," Donati said. "When's the last time you were drunk?"

"About three hours from now."

"I like that answer."

Gismondi was standing thirty yards away when Bruno and Donati exited the large brass doors. Even though he'd obtained a suppressed handgun and rifle from his contact early that morning, he had arrived at the hotel just as the inspectors were leaving. With no opportunity to kill them in their rooms, he had followed them to the Vatican. But any thought of taking a shot as they exited the archives ended abruptly when he looked around. Hiding in a secure place was both a plus and a minus. The significant distance to his targets created too much uncertainty given the number of tourists who were walking in front of them. If he was lucky, he might kill one. And even if he got close enough to pop both Bruno and Donati with his handgun, the number of Gendarmerie in the area would make his escape doubtful. With no alternative, he put his scope back in his jacket pocket, left his rifle taped to the small of his back, and returned to his vehicle.

Donati and Bruno entered their hotel and, instead of going to their rooms, went straight to the bar, where they sat at a corner table. It wasn't long before a server approached and handed both a menu, which had a wine list on the last page.

"Why don't you start us out?" Donati said, sliding his unopened menu to the right.

Bruno ignored the menu and went straight to the wine list, ordering a bottle of merlot from the Colmello di Grotta vineyard of Francesca Bortolotto Possati, owner of the Hotel Bauer in Venice. He was very familiar with the wine because it was a local favorite, and he had killed more than a few brain cells drinking it with friends. Donati, who said that he was skeptical of northern Italian wines that didn't come from the

Piedmont area, instantly became a fan of the vineyard after his first sip, and he complimented Bruno on his selection.

Once they had finished the bottle, they decided they'd better eat something if they were going to continue drinking. Bruno ordered a plate of classic risotto with black truffles, to be followed by a bone-in veal chop. Upon hearing his companion's order, Donati closed his menu and said that he'd have the same. Bruno asked Donati to order the wine that would accompany their dinner, and after consulting the wine list, Donati settled on a Pio Cesare Barolo DOCG. Bruno was excited to try his first Pio Cesare, and it didn't disappoint.

Following dinner, and after finishing the last of his wine, Bruno lit his fourth cigarette since leaving the Vatican and blew the smoke toward the ceiling.

"Those are going to kill you," Donati said. "And if that doesn't happen soon, the secondhand smoke is surely going to kill me if we continue working together."

"It's a terrible habit. And you're correct—it's not fair to those around me. I have to figure out a way to stop."

"If I can make a suggestion?"

"Please."

"Marry an insanely beautiful woman who will only make love if you don't smoke."

"That should stop me from smoking for fifteen minutes. Do you have a plan for the other twenty-three-plus hours?"

"Fifteen minutes?"

"Not even that long if it was Monica Bellucci."

Both men roared with laughter.

Donati summoned the waiter and said something to him that Bruno couldn't hear. A moment later, the waiter returned with a bottle of limoncello. The lemon liqueur went down much too smoothly, and soon the waiter removed the empty bottle and replaced it with cups of double espresso laced with Sambuca, an anise-flavored liqueur.

The two inspectors exchanged stories and laughed with one another. Both were a little unsteady, and their mental acuity was below the waves. Therefore, neither noticed the stick-thin person watching them from the patio who, twenty minutes later, made his way to their rooms.

CHAPTER 17

THE GUNSHOT WAS loud, and Donati, who had fallen sound asleep seconds after his head hit the pillow, instantly awoke. He grabbed his gun and ran to Bruno's room in his underwear and T-shirt. When he arrived, the door was wide open, and a man in a suit was kneeling over the body of Luciano Gismondi. Just inside the door were two athletic-looking men with close-cropped hair, one of whom grabbed Donati's hand holding the gun and pointed the weapon to the ground while he presented his creds. Bruno, who was also in underwear and a T-shirt, was sitting on his bed, his attention focused on Gismondi's body.

The man who was kneeling stood and said to the two officers, "Get a bag. And keep the hotel guests and staff away from this room."

Several minutes later, one of the officers returned with a body bag, into which Gismondi was unceremoniously shoved and carried from the room. The officers returned five minutes later and took positions on either side of the door. So far no guests had come out of their rooms to see what was happening.

"Shouldn't we have waited for the coroner?" Donati asked.

"There will be no coroner, photographs, or report on what occurred here," the man in the suit replied. "This piece of excrement died of a heart attack before medical attention could arrive. That will be the finding of both the coroner and the police." As he was saying this, the three men heard a hotel guest asking one of the officers in the hallway about the gunfire, and the inquiring voice of another guest soon joined. Hearing this, the man in the suit went into the hallway and spoke to both guests, saying that one of the guests had suffered a heart attack and that the sound they had heard was the gurney hitting the hallway wall as they were bringing it into the room. Neither guest questioned this.

When he returned to the room, the man introduced himself as Colonel Andrin Hunkler, commander of the pope's Swiss Guard. He was six feet, two inches tall and athletic-looking, with ramrod-straight posture and salt-and-pepper crewcut hair. He was wearing a dark gray suit, white shirt, and black-and-gray striped tie.

"Not that I'm ungrateful that you saved my life, but how did you happen to be here when the deceased broke into my room?"

"Following your visit to the pontiff's archives, His Holiness asked me to personally invite both of you to meet with him tonight. I was in the process of extending that invitation when I saw someone entering your room with a handgun. When it looked as if he was going to kill you, I took the only action possible. Do you know the deceased?"

"His name is Luciano Gismondi," Donati said. "He's a fixer for Duke Rodolfo Rizzo."

Hunkler didn't react to what he'd heard. "If you'll both throw on a pair of pants and a shirt," Hunkler said, "I have a car waiting outside."

"I'll get cleaned up and be ready in ten minutes," Donati said, starting for his room.

"You can get pretty in the car. Pants, shirt, and shoes. Let's go."

Bruno wished he'd had less to drink as he and Donati quickly got dressed and were then ushered down the hallway and through the lobby. When they walked outside, they found a Mercedes S560 waiting with its engine running. As soon as they were buckled in the back seat, the car sped toward the Vatican.

"Where's Gismondi?" Bruno asked as they sped off.

"In the trunk," Hunkler answered without turning around.

Five minutes later, they pulled up to the entrance to what looked like a hotel adjacent to St. Peter's Basilica. The colonel led them past two Swiss Guards and into the building, through several layers of additional security, and up a flight of brown carpeted stairs, worn with age, to the second floor.

"The papal apartments of past popes is across the way," the colonel explained as they walked. "The current occupant of the Throne of Saint Peter found those living quarters too opulent. Instead, he has elected to reside in suite 201 here, at the Casa Santa Marta, a residence that's traditionally been used for visiting clergy and laypeople."

"I didn't know," Bruno replied as Hunkler knocked on the door.

The entrance to room 201 was a nondescript light brown door. Written on a sign affixed to it were the words "Vietato Lamentarsi," which in Italian translated to "no complaining." Below, the sign's small print indicated that offenders "are subject to developing a victim complex, resulting in a lowering ... of their capacity to solve problems ... the penalty is doubled whenever the violation is committed in the presence of children." It went on: "To be your best you have to focus on your own potential and not on your limits, so stop whining and act to make your life better." Bruno had just finished reading this when he heard a voice from inside telling them to enter.

The pope's residence could best be described as a hotel suite consisting of two rooms—a bedroom and an office—with hardwood floors in a chevron herringbone pattern throughout. On the back wall of the office was a wooden crucifix, in front of which sat a five-foot-long wooden desk, with one chair behind and two in front. To the right and left, a large chiffonier rested against each wall. A thickly cushioned high-backed red velvet club chair sat at the back of the room, with two straight-backed wooden chairs facing it. The pope was sitting behind his desk, with Cattaneo standing at his side, when the group entered.

"Welcome," the pope said, brushing aside all formality. He stood and directed the inspectors to the two chairs at the back of the room, while he walked over and sat in the red velvet club chair across from them. Cattaneo and Hunkler stood to the pope's right.

"Marco told me about the circumstances that led to this discovery," the pontiff said, extending his hand toward his desk, on top of which were two stacks of vellum papers, along with the two pieces of paper that had seemed to cause Cattaneo so much concern. "The thick pile of papers you see are Vatican financial ledgers that are almost three centuries old. Señor Cattaneo asked our senior accountant to perform a cursory examination of them, and he has confirmed that one is an exact duplicate of the financial records of the Vatican during the papacy of Clement XII, the original of which is in my archives. The other is what I will call an alternate version of the papacy's finances for that same period. Alongside the ledgers are two letters—one from Cardinal Ettore Casaroli and the other from Duke Federigo Rizzo."

Bruno and Donati were at the edge of their seats as they listened to the pontiff, while Hunkler and Cattaneo remained expressionless.

"The letter from Cardinal Casaroli is a confession," the pope continued. "Sadly, one of the sins to which he confessed was that during both his terms as secretary of state, he and a prominent banker, Duke Federigo Rizzo, embezzled a great deal of the church's money, splitting proceeds from the sale of Vatican land and art, as well as cash donations from the faithful. Regrettably, the more money they stole, the more assets the church had to sell to fund its current operations and charitable work."

"That's one of the skeletons in the Rizzo family closet," Bruno inadvertently said to himself, but in a voice loud enough for the pope to hear.

"There are two other skeletons, to use your terminology," the pope continued. "But I'll get to those shortly. Thanks to your help, we can now document the embezzlement. I therefore intend to confront the family's current heir, Duke Rodolfo Rizzo, and demand the return of the money that his ancestors stole from the church, with interest."

"That should hurt his pocketbook," Donati said.

"I wish that the harm inflicted on the Holy See was only monetary," the pope said, "because Cardinal Casaroli's confession goes on to say that he killed Pope Clement XII with a poison that was given to him by Duke Federigo Rizzo."

Bruno and Donati looked at the pope with astonishment as he continued to speak. Hunkler and Cattaneo, however, still remained expressionless, apparently having heard this information already.

"The second letter is a note from Duke Federigo Rizzo to the cardinal, informing him that Clement had discovered their embezzlement scheme. It directs the cardinal to poison the pontiff so that they could not only retain their wealth but also avoid prison and certain excommunication."

"And the cardinal followed Rizzo's order," Bruno said.

"Lamentably. But their crimes against the church didn't end there. Cardinal Casaroli's letter goes on to say that he assisted Rizzo in his theft of church artifacts, replacing them with faithful reproductions—which is the reason you're both here. I need you to discreetly recover those artifacts without anyone knowing."

Bruno looked at Hunkler, expecting him to provide additional details, but the colonel remained stoically silent.

"Holy Father," Bruno said, "from what I've seen this evening, Colonel Hunkler and his security team are world-class. Not only did they save our lives, but they efficiently and discreetly handled the aftermath of the shooting to avoid questions about what occurred. If you have jurisdictional concerns, I believe any request from the Vatican to quietly work with Italian law enforcement would be quickly honored."

"I have no lack of confidence in the colonel, the Swiss Guard, or my Gendarmerie Corps, which, as you know, is the Vatican's primary police force. But I've been told that Duke Rodolfo Rizzo has many paid informants within law enforcement and the government. Moreover, if either the Swiss Guard or the Gendarmerie were discovered taking the action I'm contemplating, it would have a serious impact on the image of the church. That's because what I'm asking you and Inspector Donati to do is break the law."

"Meaning that if we're caught trying to repatriate the church's artifacts, we're two thieves attempting to steal these artifacts for personal gain. And if we're successful, what we did will forever remain a secret."

"An astute and precise summary," the pope replied.

Bruno gave Hunkler a look that said he believed the colonel was the author of the plan that the pope was presenting, because whoever had put this together seemed to be stretching the ethical envelope.

"Can you tell us what the artifacts are? And do you possibly have photographs?" Donati asked, tacitly giving his approval.

"There's a replica of one of the items behind my desk," the pope said, pointing to the cross hanging on the wall.

Bruno and Donati's jaws dropped in unison.

They were on their way to St. Peter's, where Hunkler had sent several Swiss Guards ahead to unlock the basilica, which had been secured for the evening, and to turn on the lights. By the time they arrived, the doors were standing open, and they proceeded to the confession area, the niche to the rear of the Papal Altar. There they descended a marble staircase to the Vatican Grottoes, where many popes, as well as a few royals from as far back as the tenth century, were buried.

Continuing their descent to the next subterranean level, they passed through the Vatican Necropolis, a Pagan and Christian burial ground built on Vatican Hill between 27 BC and AD 476, and walked down a slanted pathway that took them from sixteen to forty feet below the basilica floor. They continued to what the pontiff referred to as Field P, which contained a small earthen mound with a hole dug out of it, said to contain the bones of Saint Peter. The pope genuflected in front of it. Adjacent to the mound was an old door. The pope unbuttoned the top three buttons of his white cassock, removed a gold chain holding a key from around his neck, and opened the door. While Hunkler and Cattaneo waited, the pope hit a light switch and led Bruno and Donati inside.

The ornate chapel they entered had twenty-foot-high walls, extending fifty feet on each side. The walls were covered in mosaics, accentuated by a background of gold glass tesserae, which depicted the fourteen Stations of the Cross and the resurrection of Jesus. At the front of the room was a simple white marble altar, and lying on the floor behind it were three crosses. The center one was raised several feet above the rest. Each cross was enclosed in an airtight transparent enclosure, the one in the center being taller and thicker than the others. Protruding from the enclosure was a plastic tube which connected to a cylinder containing inert gas. Stepping closer to the center cross, Bruno and Donati saw that a wooden plaque with an inscription was attached to the top: "Jesus Nazaranus Rex Iudaeorum."

On the altar, also enclosed within a gas-sealed transparent enclosure, was a crown of thorns made from the *Euphorbia milii* plant—historically used by the Romans because it was supple enough to be made into a crown. Alongside it were three iron nails, known as crucifixion spikes, measuring five feet, three-quarter inches in length.

Bruno and Donati were speechless.

"These are replicas of what's been stolen," the pope said. "Through the ages, access to this room was given only to the bishop of Rome and his secretary of state. Once a cardinal ascends to the Throne of Saint Peter, he is given a letter by the prefect of the Vatican Secret Archives providing the location of the chapel and an explanation of what is contained within. Enclosed with the letter is the access key. The pope then shares this information with his newly appointed secretary of state. I requested that the prefect retrieve the key prior to your arrival."

Bruno and Donati had trouble taking their eyes off the three crosses, even though they knew they were replicas.

"According to the cardinal's letter," the pope continued, "the duke learned about the chapel when both men were at his estate and the cardinal had gotten quite drunk. Publicly, the duke was a devout Catholic, because at that time anyone who wasn't would have been ostracized from essentially all social and business relationships. But privately, he admitted to the cardinal that he was an atheist with no belief in an afterlife."

"Then why would he want these relics?" Bruno asked.

"The cardinal's letter never provided a reason. It said only that the duke had blackmailed him by buying up his gambling markers, which were apparently substantial. If he helped steal these sacred relics and replace them with fakes, then the duke would destroy his markers."

"When did someone notice these weren't real?" Donati asked.

"They didn't. Remember, Clement was blind, and if he did visit the True Cross, he would have been accompanied by Cardinal Casaroli. That gave the duke almost a decade to make exact replicas. After Clement died, everyone who came here accepted on faith that these relics were authentic because only the two most senior individuals in the church knew about and could enter this chapel. The three crosses were placed within inert gas enclosures in the 1950s, with the assistance of several clergy. Thereafter, the gas pressure was monitored by the secretary of state."

As the pope led them back upstairs, Bruno turned to Donati. "Do you have any idea how we can get onto the patriarch's heavily guarded estate, which is probably where's he's keeping the relics, and steal three large crosses along with the other relics, then escape alive?"

"All but the last part," Donati answered.

CHAPTER 18

THE PLAN FOR getting onto the patriarch's Bellagio property was a matter of using common sense. It was well known that the duke rarely left his estate, but when he did, it was usually to go to one of Milan's phenomenal Michelin three-star restaurants. But dinner at Acquolina, one of the top ten restaurants in the world, which had only twenty-three tables, had always eluded him. The chef and owner, who had grown up poor, took great delight in turning down reservations for those who thought they had enough money and influence to get into any restaurant. Thus, the patriarch had never been allowed to dine there, a fact that was well known throughout the city and that created a great deal of animosity between Duke Rizzo and the chef. But once Bruno and Donati approached the owner and explained that they were investigating the patriarch and needed to keep Rizzo at his restaurant for as close to four hours as possible, the owner agreed to cooperate and extend an invitation to the patriarch. The chef never asked either inspector what they were investigating, but Bruno credited him with believing that any investigation was unlikely to be in the duke's best interest.

So while Bruno and Donati stood beside him, the chef phoned the patriarch and extended an invitation for him to dine at his establishment at eight o'clock that evening. He also heightened Rizzo's anticipation by noting that he would be preparing him a special meal that was not on the menu. The patriarch never questioned the reason for his invitation. Instead, he accepted it with a great deal of false humility, and at seven fifteen, he left the estate for dinner.

After receiving a call from the restaurant's chef reporting that Duke Rizzo had arrived, Bruno told Donati that they were clear to dock. With Donati at the oars, the small rowboat moved effortlessly in the glass-like water as it slowly approached the boathouse. The large structure, which seemed more fitting for commercial rather than personal use, was 150 feet wide and 100 feet deep and stood twenty feet high. It had three exterior piers, each leading to a steel door that touched the surface of the lake. The inspectors docked and tied up at the pier farthest to their left. Bruno, who'd been smoking a cigarette, drew one last puff into his lungs before throwing the butt into the placid water and followed Donati onto the pier.

They planned to breach the estate through what they considered its most vulnerable access point. They had arrived at this conclusion for several reasons. The first was that it was detached from the main building and therefore probably had weaker security. The second was that they believed, given the duke's penchant for privacy, that there had to be a tunnel between the two structures. Reinforcing this belief was the fact that Google Earth showed no road or walkway connecting the two buildings. Bruno and Donati didn't believe that the duke was tearing up his pristine lawn to send a vehicle down to the water every time a boat was launched. But both agreed that if their assumption was incorrect, then they'd have no choice but to trudge up the hill and find some other way to enter the mansion undetected. Neither looked forward to that scenario.

Each man wore a wetsuit and a snorkel and had a waterproof bag slung across his back as the pair lowered themselves into the water. They silently resurfaced within the boathouse alongside a classic mahogany motorboat that was tied to one of the three interior piers, with the other two piers having variations of the same boat alongside them.

They eventually came to a set of concrete steps that led onto the surrounding deck, and after drying themselves off with towels taken from their waterproof bags, they changed into all-black attire—slacks, turtlenecks, and athletic footwear. Each then put on a shoulder holster containing a Beretta 92FS handgun with suppressor, compliments of Donati's home armory. In front of them appeared to be the tunnel entrance they'd been looking for, protected by a steel door displaying the Rizzo family seal. The problem was that neither could figure out how to open it.

With the deaths of Gismondi and Sartori, the next in line to be the duke's senior security supervisor was an ex-mafia thug named Giulio Negri. The forty-year-old Sicilian was a brawler from Palermo who loved to break body parts as a way of making his point and getting what he wanted. Those who worked with him tended to joke behind his back that if he were shot in the head, no harm would come to him because there was nothing but a vacuum inside.

The duke left for the restaurant with all but Negri and seven members of the security staff, who remained behind to guard the estate. Since the patriarch wasn't in residence, he decided to take advantage of the situation and go down to the boathouse to delve into the case of Ketel One that he had purloined from one of the duke's parties. With no shortage of volunteers to accompany him, since Negri's stash was an open secret among the guards, he picked two to follow him, promising those who remained that they'd get their chance before the duke returned.

Negri and the two guards took the elevator from the main floor of the mansion down to the garage level, where they got into a golf cart. Negri was driving. He touched a button on a remote control affixed to the steering wheel, and a steel door slid aside and exposed a long tunnel, with LED lighting along its sides. The tunnel, which had a moderate slope because it ran nearly half a mile from the mansion to the edge of the lake floor, was made from a nonslip polymer that had numerous drains in it to funnel water seepage into the lake.

Fifty feet from the end of the tunnel, which terminated at a steel door emblazoned with the duke's crest, the cart broke an electronic beam, and the door before them slid back into a recess. As they entered the boathouse, the interior transformed from its dim default lighting to that mimicking daylight.

Bruno and Donati were standing in front of the sliding steel door when the overhead lights suddenly brightened. Fortunately, because of the weight of the door, it took a few seconds for the slab of steel to slide into its recess. This gave them time to grab their bags and take cover behind a storage container just before a golf cart with three men aboard entered and the steel door slid shut behind them.

The first person out of the cart was the driver, a barrel-chested man who appeared to be in his early forties, with salt-and-pepper hair, and stood five feet nine in height. His face was deeply pockmarked, which made him look ten years older than he was. Bruno and Donati stood motionless as they watched the man walk to the lip of the pier they'd just swum beside and begin pulling on a rope that extended into the water. Soon a net containing six bottles of Ketel One vodka broke the surface, and he hoisted it onto the deck. Taking one bottle from the net, he returned the rest to the cold water.

Bottle in hand, the man then stepped off the pier and onto the boat, where he was joined by the other two guards who'd accompanied him. Bruno and Donati heard one of the guards address the man as Negri. Soon he was pouring generous portions into glasses that bore the duke's family crest. With the three men having a grand time on the boat, Bruno and Donati were able to whisper to one another without fear of being overheard.

"I don't think we have enough time to wait until they get inebriated—if they do," Donati said.

"Agreed. And four hours isn't much time to subdue the security staff, find what we're looking for, and repatriate the stolen items. Given the size of the mansion, we'll need every second," Bruno said. "I'll approach from stern and you the bow."

Donati nodded in agreement.

With guns drawn, they silently approached and stepped onto the boat before Negri looked up and saw them. None of the three men were rocket scientists, but with two guns pointing at them, they knew they had no chance of survival if they reached for their weapons. Therefore, at Bruno's urging, each man slowly removed his gun from his shoulder holster and dropped it into the water.

While Bruno kept his gun trained on the guards, Donati found a roll of braided cotton rope and duct tape in a storage bin. He then had each man empty his pockets before he tied their hands behind their backs and bound their feet with the rope, after which he placed a strip of duct tape over everyone's mouth but Negri's, since the other two men's deference toward him indicated that he was the leader.

Grabbing Negri by the arm, Bruno dragged him off the boat and onto the deck, getting far enough away that the other two men couldn't hear what was being said. "How many men are standing guard tonight?" Bruno asked.

Negri answered with silence and a venomous look in his eyes.

"Here's what's going to happen. You're the only one who hasn't been gagged, and I'm talking to you. Your two fellow scumbags can see this. My guess is that neither likes you. Therefore, I'm going to walk you back to your two friends, put my arm around you, and tell you that the monetary reward for your cooperation can be picked up tomorrow morning in Milan. I'll sound very convincing. You'll deny it, but they won't believe you because they don't want to. How long do you think it will take the patriarch to kill you? Even if he isn't sure that you've turned on him, he'll still murder you, because why take a chance with the hired help? You're expendable; he's not."

The expression on Negri's face transformed from rage to denial and finally acceptance. "There's five men in the house," Negri said.

"Have them come here," Bruno ordered.

Negri did.

Ten minutes later, the five guards entered the boathouse aboard two carts. The looks on their faces indicated that the last thing they had expected to see was two men pointing guns at them. After the five men were disarmed and searched, they were tied up and gagged. Each of the eight guards was then secured to a separate support pillar within the boathouse so that they couldn't work together to untie themselves. And thanks to a cooperative Negri, who probably realized he'd given too much cooperation to back out, Bruno and Donati now knew how to get into the mansion.

The fifteen-foot-wide north–south corridor that ran the length of the mansion was steps from the elevator. Donati, who was familiar with the building's layout, having been to the estate on a number of occasions, said that he'd search the south end of the mansion and for Bruno to take the north, which ended at a set of ten-foot-tall bronze doors.

Just as the immense boathouse had seemed incongruous for a residential structure, the enormous bronze doors that sealed the north end of the mansion seemed better suited to a cathedral than a residence, since each door was inlaid with five intricate vertical panels depicting events in the life of Christ. Judging from the time and money it must have taken to construct the doors and given their religious theme, Bruno excitedly believed he just might have found where the Rizzo family had been hiding the stolen Vatican relics for so many centuries.

Because there were no obvious handles or keyholes, Bruno pushed on the giant doors to see if they were unlocked. They didn't budge. Fifteen minutes later, after searching the doors for a secret access panel or hidden keyhole, he had still come up empty. As he stepped away to see if viewing the doors at a distance would expose something he hadn't seen, he noticed a tall silk plant five feet from the door. In a home where everything was extremely high-end and pristine, the artificial plant had the look of a McDonald's hamburger on a gourmet tasting menu—it was obviously out of place. Pulling the plant aside, Bruno found what he was looking for. That was the good news. The bad was that it was an RFID reader, which he had no idea how to bypass. Twenty minutes later, he was still staring at it when Donati approached from his right.

"I found something very interesting in the patriarch's study," said Donati.

"What'd you find?" Bruno asked, finally turning his back on the security device.

"A button on the underside of his desk drawer. When I pressed it, the wall behind his desk recessed and exposed a huge vault door. I'm talking about something you might see in a bank. Interestingly, there's an RFID reader to the right of it, not dissimilar from the one you were just staring at," Donati said. "As an FYI, I also took a quick look at the duke's office. There's nothing of interest there."

"Then we both have the same problem—bypassing an RFID entry system. My guess is that what we're looking for is behind these doors or inside the vault," Bruno said.

"Agreed."

"Go outside and see if there's another way to get into the area on the other side of these doors. Perhaps there's an outside door that's a weaker entry point. If not, then I may have to resort to something that could get us into a great deal of trouble."

"More than breaking into the home of the wealthiest and most influential person in Italy without a warrant and tying and gagging eight of his security staff?"

"Good point."

The north end of the mansion was a rectangular extension of the building that ended in a turret. There was no doubt that it was a chapel because there were fourteen faceted stained-glass windows, seven on a side, depicting the Stations of the Cross. The three-story-high turret at the end had a circular stained-glass window in the center showing the resurrection of Christ. The interior of the structure was apparently lit, spectacularly illuminating the stained glass at night. But much to Donati's dismay, there was no exterior entry door. When he returned inside, he saw Bruno standing exactly where he'd left him.

"There's a large chapel on the other side of these doors, but there's no exterior entry door," Donati said. "It's probably time to implement your idea."

CHAPTER 19

REGINA COELI WAS constructed as a convent in 1654 and became a prison in 1881 when it was abandoned by the Carmelite nuns. Indro Montanari, who had begun his life as a thief at the tender age of twelve, was now a resident of that facility for a minimum of five years and a maximum of ten years thanks to Chief Inspector Mauro Bruno.

Montanari was not your run-of-the-mill smash-and-dash intruder. His specialty was electronically bypassing sophisticated electronic entry systems that were marketed as impossible to get around. Disproving the impossible had earned him a fortune until the day Mauro Bruno, holding two cups of espresso, entered the rare coin dealer's vault he was robbing. Of course, there had been a legion of Polizia di Stato standing directly behind the chief inspector. That was the day Montanari found out that he needed glasses, because he'd touched the wrong contact on the cipher lock's circuit board and set off a silent alarm. Having entered prison at the age of thirty, he now had three more years to serve before he would become eligible for parole.

Montanari was sitting on his thinly padded bed, wearing a pair of glasses that the government had generously given him, and reading a contraband book on electrical circuitry when he heard a guard approaching. Placing the book under the mattress, he pretended to be sleeping when the guard came to his cell.

"Wake up, Montanari. You have a call," the guard said.

Since calling privileges were limited to a defined time of day, which had already passed, and no incoming calls of any type were permitted to inmates, Montanari was confused and didn't move.

The guard signaled for someone at the end of the row of cells to open Montanari's door and then pulled the thirty-two-year-old prisoner off his bed and cuffed him. Montanari was taken to a private room in the administrative wing of the prison and handed a cell phone—which, from the look on the warden's face as he walked past the prisoner, must have belonged to the warden himself.

Once the door closed and he was by himself, Montanari asked who he was speaking to. When he heard that it was Bruno, he was genuinely pleased to talk with the chief inspector, to whom he'd taken an immediate liking from the moment he'd handed him an espresso in the vault. It wasn't Bruno's fault that they had opposite professions. After a brief hello, Bruno got straight to the point.

"Indro, I'm in a hurry, and I need your help. I want to bypass an RFID reader, and I need you to tell me how I can do that without setting off an alarm."

"You want me to tell you how to do exactly what got me arrested?" Montanari asked, not believing what he was hearing.

"Exactly. If you help me, and this leads to what I think it will, I'll see if I can get your sentence commuted."

Montanari didn't need a second invitation. He hated every day of his prison life. "Go to the RFID pad and give me the model number," he said.

Five minutes later, after following Montanari's instructions, which involved two paper clips and a pocketknife that Donati had taken from the duke's office, Bruno heard a loud click come from the bronze doors and saw the light on the RFID pad change from red to green.

"Thank you, Indro," Bruno said. "If we're successful, I won't forget our agreement." He then terminated the call.

With Donati following, Bruno approached the bronze doors. Though large and presumably heavy, they moved inward with only slight pressure from his hand. The ten-thousand-square-foot interior had black marble flooring throughout. In the center was a gold altar, flanked on either side by a golden angel, each with its hands outstretched toward the altar. There were no pews or a viewing area. Instead, in front of the altar there was a single thickly padded black leather chair.

Walking into the dimly lit chapel, Bruno removed a flashlight from his waterproof bag and pointed it at the altar and the angels to get a better look. He then scratched their surfaces with his fingernail. "I think the altar and the angels are solid gold," Bruno said. "Given their size, there must be several tons of gold here."

Donati also scratched the gold surfaces of each and agreed with Bruno. "Why have this room for a family that, according to Cardinal Casaroli, is atheist? It makes no sense. Why not melt the gold and cast it into bars, then put it in a Swiss bank?" Donati asked, taking a seat in the black padded chair.

"Gold is a commodity. It would be easier to transport and far easier to sell if it was in that form."

"I don't believe this chapel ever had a religious significance for the Rizzo family. I think it was constructed for appearances," said Bruno. "When this was built, the Catholic Church was the dominant social and economic force in Italy, and there was little if any separation between one's religious, business, and personal lives. Having this opulent chapel, with the magnificent stained-glass windows and the gold altar and angels, gave the outward appearance of the Rizzo family's extreme devotion to the church. It cemented their family's position in the community."

"I agree with everything you just said," Donati replied. "But more to the point, I don't see what we're looking for inside this chapel."

Bruno took a deep breath and rubbed his weary eyes for a few seconds. "The RFID system outside the chapel is apparently there to protect the gold."

"While the one in the duke's study must be protecting something of similar or greater value," Donati said.

"Exactly."

Closing the chapel doors behind them, they ran down the corridor to Rizzo's study.

The lights within the cell area of the Regina Coeli prison were turned off from ten at night until six in the morning, so Indro Montanari was reading his book using a small flashlight when he again heard footsteps approaching his cell. Hiding his book, he faked being asleep as a guard yelled to another officer to unlock his cell.

Pissed off because he had again been summoned to a prisoner's cell when he should have been relaxing in the break room and smoking a cigarette, the guard toughly pulled Montanari out of bed and tightened his handcuffs a little more than necessary before ushering him out of his cell and back to the administrative wing.

When the warden again handed Montanari his cell phone, the look on his face indicated that he'd rather have given the person who'd put a hole in his evening a cigarette and a blindfold rather than his phone. After the warden and the guard left the office and closed the door behind them, as Bruno had instructed them to do, Montanari again asked the chief inspector what he wanted. What he heard caused him to let out an involuntary gasp.

"This RFID pad may look the same as the other, but they're a universe apart in sophistication," said Montanari. "The last RFID reader was primary school. This is graduate studies. It's an unforgiving system—meaning any error triggers a silent alarm."

"I understand. Nevertheless, I need to get inside this vault. Can you help me?"

Montanari's answer was instantaneous. If there was a chance in a thousand that he could get out of prison three years early, he was going to take it. "I'll give you a list of items you'll need to hack the system. Once you obtain them, I'll take you step by step through a series of procedures. You cannot deviate even slightly from what you're told. If you don't fully understand what I'm saying, then stop me, and I'll go over it again."

Bruno said he understood, and Montanari gave him the list. Donati then gathered the supplies, which included several strands of wire stripped from a lamp in addition to the two paper clips and pocketknife.

Bruno removed the plastic cover from the RFID pad, just as he had done with the one outside the chapel, and then unhinged the circuit board. With Donati holding the circuit board with one hand and the cell phone to Bruno's ear with the other, Montanari began giving step-by-step instructions. Ten minutes after they started, Bruno heard a click and saw the light on the circuit board transition from red to green. Montanari then helped him sequentially remove the strands of wire and two paperclips before reassembling the RFID reader. Once this was done, Bruno ended the call, and he and Donati entered the vault.

CHAPTER 20

THE VAULT TURNED out to be a large room lined with thick wooden shelves. Stored on these half-inch-thick pieces of mahogany were black leather–bound books, with dates etched in gold leaf on the outside spines. The first book was dated 1724, and the last had the current year written on it. The shelves extended two-thirds of the way down both the left and right walls. In the center of the vault, there was a descending white marble staircase with a golden handrail bordering it. At the rear of the vault was what appeared to be a very large freight elevator. The interior of the vault and the stairs were well lit, and Bruno and Donati took the stairs to the next level down, which was ten feet below the room with the thick mahogany shelves.

The remove below appeared to be approximately three times the size of the room above them, although they couldn't see the entire area because their view was partially blocked by the large steel enclosure housing the freight elevator. The interior was in sharp contrast to the room above, in that it lacked any ornateness. Every surface was faced with concrete and covered in what looked to be a thick waterproof sealant. Bruno saw a set of electronic controls on the wall to his right. The labels above them indicated that one was for temperature and the other for humidity. The interior lighting consisted of the same LED strips that he'd seen on the first level of the vault, minus any decorative covering.

As he and Donati walked past the edge of the elevator, and the entire room came into view, they momentarily froze: there, less than ten feet in front of them, three crosses laid side by side on the concrete floor. Walking closer, they noticed that the center cross differed from the other two. Attached to the top of it by a piece of old rope was a wooden plaque with an inscription: "Jesus Nazaranus Rex Iudaeorum." Each cross was stored inside a rigidly constructed transparent enclosure, similar to what they'd seen at the Vatican. Bruno assumed that each of the enclosures was pressurized with inert gas, since there was a small metal connector protruding from each case. Adjacent to the crosses were the crown of thorns and three iron crucifixion spikes, which were also housed in a transparent display. To the right of the holy relics and against the back wall of the room were six hydraulic lifts.

"Looks like we've found what we came for," Donati said. "And just as you predicted, the equipment to lift and move them is nearby."

"It was more a guess than a prediction," Bruno confessed. "Before we do anything, let's take a quick look at what's written in the books upstairs. I'm curious as to why they require the same security as the crosses."

When they reentered the main floor of the vault, Bruno grabbed the black book from the most current year while Donati selected the one dated 1724. They carried their respective books into Rizzo's study, sat down in two chairs, and began reading.

Bruno and Donati agreed that they had a solid two and possibly two and a half hours before the patriarch would return to the estate. They'd take a quick glance at a couple of books, then bring the crosses and other relics up the elevator and out of the vault and transport them in one or two of the duke's trucks or vans. They didn't have to transport them far, only to a nearby pasture, where Hunkler had helicopters and men ready to fly them to the Vatican. They acknowledged that the primary weakness in their plan, which they had no control over since they couldn't exactly drive an eighteen-wheeler to the front door of Rizzo's estate, would be finding something large enough to transport the relics. Failing that, Bruno and Donati planned to use the hydraulic lifts to place the relics individually onto the roof of a large vehicle, strap them down, and transport them one by one to Hunkler. They figured they'd need an hour and a half max to make that happen.

Bruno would have preferred that Hunkler land his helicopters on the patriarch's lawn and that Swiss Guards help them transport the relics off the estate. But they both knew that wasn't going to happen because if things went south, Bruno and Donati needed to take the fall so that the Vatican would stay out of the picture. In keeping with that scenario, Hunkler was giving them until 12:30 a.m., four and a half hours after the duke began his dinner, to get to the landing zone before the helicopters would return to Rome without them. Any later, and the duke would be back at his estate, and the game would be over.

Failure wasn't an option in anyone's mind because everyone realized that if the duke discovered his secret was out, they'd never get a second opportunity to recover the relics; Rizzo would immediately have them moved. And with his resources, it was safe to say that no one would ever find them again after that.

Bruno opened the book he was holding and began reading the last entry in the duke's diary. Ten minutes later, he called to Donati. "I have what amounts to a confession from Rizzo that he ordered the deaths of my father, the mayor, and others after a monk accidentally discovered the ledgers we learned about at the Vatican."

"That would normally give us the evidence we need to arrest him," Donati said. "And it would be impossible for him to refute his own confession, except ..."

"We're inside his home illegally," Bruno continued, finishing the sentence. "Therefore, no judge will let us use this evidence in court. Legally, our proof doesn't exist."

"As an FYI," Donati said, "the diary I'm reading documents how Cardinal Casaroli worked with Duke Federigo Rizzo to systematically embezzle money, land, art, and anything else of value from the Vatican. Those funds became the basis for the Rizzo family fortune. It's all here in Rodolfo's ancestor's handwriting. That begs the question—why would anyone keep a handwritten record of their crimes, especially murder?"

"Arrogance and a feeling of invulnerability that comes with what they believe is absolute power. How many times have we seen that sense of entitlement in some of the rich and powerful that we've arrested?" Bruno asked.

Donati nodded in agreement. "I guess this is one way to pass on the family history between generations."

"From what we know, the relics aren't religiously significant to the Rizzos. So again, why do it? In the eighteenth century, if what Federigo had done had come to light, he would have lost everything. Why not just construct his chapel and pretend to be a good Catholic?"

"This entry might explain some of that," Donati said, and he began to read aloud what Duke Federigo Rizzo had written nearly three hundred years earlier.

Today the replicas have passed their final test. The two artisans I employed produced perfect copies that fooled, I'm told, even the fastidious Pope Benedict XIII. For two years, under Cardinal Casaroli's direction, these craftsmen made drawings, took measurements of the relics, and finely crafted these duplicates. But keeping these craftsmen alive beyond this point was an unacceptable risk, and I had Casaroli dispatch both once I knew their work could pass the scrutiny of the pontiff.

Casaroli once asked me why I must have the church's most sacred and prized possessions, as they are too well known to sell or display, and secrecy is paramount if I am to avoid the consequences of this theft. My response startled him—I want what the church considers the bedrock of its existence. If my embezzlement of church assets is discovered, what better way to secretly barter for my exoneration than by having its most sacred possessions?

"It was his insurance policy," Bruno said. Looking at his watch, he stood and approached Donati. "We've technically got an hour and a half before Rizzo returns. Let's find a vehicle."

Bruno and Donati took the elevator to the garage and looked closely at the sea of cars before them, something they should have done earlier because the largest vehicle they could see was an SUV.

"I guess we're going with plan B. Let's take three of the SUVs to the front of the mansion and use the hydraulic lifts to put them onto the roof of each vehicle," Bruno said.

Donati agreed, and they dashed back to the lower level of the vault and tried to roll two of the portable hydraulic lifts to the center cross. Unfortunately, at this point they noticed that not only were the tires on these two lifts flat, but so were the tires on the other four.

"It's probably been years since these lifts were used and their tires filled with air," Donati said.

They both stood silent for a moment before concluding that it was time to pack it in and leave the estate before the duke returned. As they walked up the stairway and into the top level of the vault, Donati stopped and looked around. "I have an idea about how we can get the relics."

Bruno looked inquisitively at him.

"We take these diaries and broker a trade with Rizzo. We'll return them in exchange for the relics. He won't want the information in these books to be made public. It would not only destroy his reputation but also ruin the public's trust in his bank. Think of it—who'd want to do business with someone whose fortune is built on money embezzled from the Vatican? Over and above that, the relics are now a liability since we know of their existence. He can't afford to turn our offer down. There's one major problem, however. If we do this, he gets away with multiple homicides, including your father's." Donati looked at Bruno closely. "Will you be all right with that?"

"No. But I'll address that issue on my own. But you know that he's going to send someone to kill us after he gets the diaries back," Bruno said.

"I'd expect nothing less from this dirtbag."

"Then get the biggest SUV in the garage and drive it to the front door," Bruno said, "while I leave Rizzo a calling card and then start bringing the diaries outside."

Donati found a GMC Yukon XL in the garage and drove it to the front of the mansion just as Bruno was coming out with his second armful of books. As large as the vehicle was, they needed every inch of space and even had to stack several books on each of their laps to take every diary.

After leaving the estate, they set off for a safe house in Milan, which Donati had used several times to hide witnesses from the mafia. On the way there, Bruno called Hunkler's cell and told him that their current mission was canceled. He asked the colonel to give him a call on a landline when he got to Rome so that Bruno could explain the new plan that he and Donati had just initiated. Bruno then provided the safe house's number, which Donati had given him, and hung up. Although the colonel didn't seem thrilled, he acknowledged what he'd been told. Five minutes later, Bruno and Donati heard four large helicopters passing overhead.

CHAPTER 21

T HE DUKE SUSPECTED something was up when his vehicle approached the front door of the mansion and Negri wasn't there to personally greet him—something the head of security routinely did when Rizzo returned to the property. Upon walking inside, he should have seen one or more of his staff or heard them playing their childish video games. Instead, there was nothing but silence. A subsequent search of the mansion by the guards who had accompanied him to the restaurant revealed that none of his security staff were inside. Directing them to search the property, he went to his study to retrieve his gun, which he kept in his desk drawer. But he never laid a finger on it because sitting in the center of his otherwise clear desk was a note.

We have your family diaries and will trade them for the stolen relics stored inside your vault. The exchange will take place at your estate at 3:00 p.m. tomorrow. Three large rental trucks will drive onto your property, and the men in them will retrieve the relics from the vault and place them in the vehicles. Once these trucks are safely off the estate, and we know that they are not being followed, we'll provide the location of the diaries. If you try anything, we'll deliver these books to the press, along with the two financial ledgers. Yes, we have a copy of them, and they should make interesting reading for the bank's shareholders.

Even though the note was unsigned, there was no doubt in Rizzo's mind as to who'd invaded his home.

He pressed the button under his desk, and the rear wall of his study retreated into its recess. Outwardly, the vault seemed to be secure. He then looked for the RFID card in his wallet and saw that it was in the slot where he always kept it. Removing the card from his wallet, he pressed it to the RFID reader, and the vault door immediately opened.

Rizzo's stature was generally erect; he didn't slouch, and he walked and stood as if at military attention. Some said he looked as if he'd had a stick shoved up his nether regions. But when he saw that the shelves inside the vault were empty, his knees buckled, and his posture became stooped—three centuries of his family's deepest and darkest secrets were in the hands of strangers. Rizzo didn't know how they'd bypassed the RFID system and gotten inside the vault. Nevertheless, the damage was done. Walking downstairs to where the relics were stored, he saw that everything seemed undisturbed.

"There's no one in the garage," said one of the guards as he entered the study, "but the Yukon is missing. We'll check the boathouse."

"I'll come with you," Rizzo said, following him out of the room.

The garage had assigned spaces for three golf carts. When Rizzo stepped off the elevator, he noticed that only one cart was there, and it was parked between two of the spaces, something none of his staff would have done.

"I believe I know where I can find my new security staff," Rizzo said as he got into the passenger seat of the golf cart.

When they reached the boathouse, Rizzo saw that his security staff had been tied up and gagged. Without saying a word, the patriarch pulled a gun from the hands of one of the guards accompanying him and slowly and meticulously killed each of the eight men who'd disappointed him. He saved the last bullets in the clip for Negri, who'd been in charge that evening. When he was through, he ordered their bodies to be weighted down and dropped into the deepest part of the lake.

Upon landing in Rome, Hunkler went to the airport's operations center and returned Bruno's call. The chief inspector gave him a brief overview of what had happened at the estate, including the fact that he and Donati had seen the relics in question. Hunkler, who had told the pope he was skeptical of Bruno and Donati's ability to find the church's stolen property, now had a total reversal of confidence in the two inspectors. He listened intently as Bruno provided the details for the exchange, along with a request for support materials, equipment, and manpower.

Walking back to the helicopters, Hunkler told the pilots not to get too comfortable because they would be taking off at ten and going back to Bellagio. He then returned to the operations center and made several other phone calls, arranging for the men he needed as well as the rental trucks that Bruno had requested. When he left the airport at four that morning, he intended to go straight to his apartment within the Vatican, get a few hours of sleep, and then shower and shave before returning to the Ciampino airport. Those plans went out the window when he received a call from the pope asking him to come to his room at the Casa Santa Marta at five and give him an update.

Four Italian army ICH-47F Chinook helicopters, twin-rotor behemoths capable of carrying up to fifty-five men each, lifted off from the Ciampino airport at exactly 10:00 a.m. and set down two hours later on the same patch of grass that they'd left a half day earlier. Hunkler, temporarily placed in charge of all Vatican forces by the pope, ordered the thirty Gendarmerie from his helicopter, along with twenty others from another Chinook, to off-load the shock-reduction packing materials, portable lifts, and various other items his staff had obtained from various merchants that they'd awoken in the middle of the night. While this was going on, he took four guards to a waiting taxi service van, which he'd summoned while airborne, and gave the driver the address of a truck rental agency in Milan.

At 3:00 p.m. four rental trucks arrived at the gates of the patriarch's estate and, finding the gates open, continued up the long driveway to the front of the mansion. Waiting for them on the gravel driveway outside were three crosses, a crown of thorns, and crucifixion spikes, all within their enclosures. Although the patriarch wasn't present, four of his guards watched as the Gendarmerie enveloped each relic's container with shock-absorbing packing before loading them onto the vehicles. The trucks departed the mansion forty-five minutes after their arrival and headed back to the helicopter landing site.

Once the relics were on board the helicopters and secured, Bruno, Donati, and Hunkler boarded a Chinook, and they all lifted off. Four Gendarmerie remained behind to return the trucks to the rental agency. Afterward, they'd take a train back to the Vatican.

The patriarch watched from the window of his study, his intense anger reflected in the grinding of his teeth and narrowing of his eyes, as the giant Chinooks slowly faded in the distance. Not long ago, he'd received a text from Bruno indicating that his diaries were on his boathouse dock. His men were now on their way to retrieve them. But the books would not remain in Milan for long. By this time tomorrow, they'd be on their way to a much more secure location.

Rizzo was angry for two reasons, which converged into the perfect storm. The first was that he'd forfeited the relics and therefore his bargaining chip with the church in the event his family's indiscretions came to light. The second was that every patriarch for the past three hundred years had protected what he'd just lost, and today he'd betrayed that generational trust. The restaurant had obviously been the perfect setup, and Rizzo planned to address that deception with the owner at the appropriate time. Today, however, he was focused on enacting his revenge on the two individuals he believed responsible for his present circumstances—Bruno and Donati. Unfortunately, he had only four security staff remaining, none of whom he believed had the creativity or talent necessary to kill them. He had no intention of leaving Bruno and Donati's fate to amateurs. He and the *capofamiglia* in Milan had received and provided services to one another throughout the years, and today Rizzo decided it was his turn to request a favor—for a price. Always for a price. Removing his cell phone from his pocket, he dialed a number that he'd long ago memorized.

The four Chinooks landed at the Ciampino airport, a 10.2-mile drive from the Vatican. Upon their arrival, four military tactical logistics vehicles were waiting, their enclosed truck beds covered with thick mattresses. Hunkler supervised the transfer of the relics, which were covered in thick blue tarps, from the helicopters to the trucks and rode in the lead vehicle as the caravan made its way to a side entrance of St. Peter's. Earlier, the entire square had been cordoned off by movable steel barricades that prevented anyone from getting anywhere near the basilica. Signs attached to those barricades announced that the area was closed due to an upgrade of the security system. As a result, Hunkler and the Gendarmerie had the time and space to do what they needed and remain unseen.

Prior to assuming their duties at the Vatican, all members of the Gendarmerie had taken an oath that they would not divulge anything that they might hear or see while on duty. Each man who wore the uniform had competed for the few openings that were annually available; they were required to be of good moral and ethical character and to be pious Catholics. Hunkler knew that even though these men clearly saw what they were carrying into the basilica and down the steps to an unknown door near Field P, none would ever discuss it, even among themselves. Their oath, honor, and loyalty to the pope wouldn't permit it.

As the True Cross and the other relics were being removed from the trucks, half of Hunkler's men, led by Cattaneo, were retrieving the fake relics and transferring them to vehicles. The pope had decided that the fakes should be secretly stored in a remote Vatican warehouse to which only the pontiff and the prefect of the Vatican archives would have access, confessing to Hunkler that he didn't want to destroy even copies of the most sacred relics in the church. He'd leave a letter for future pontiffs and let them make their own decisions regarding the future of the replicas.

Originally, two huge monumental towers were supposed to have been built beside St. Peter's Basilica. In 1638 construction was begun on these towers by Gian Lorenzo Bernini, the architect most notably associated with, among his many accomplishments, the design of St. Peter's Square. But as they rose, the ground beneath them proved to be unstable, and in 1643 work was halted. Therefore, they never got higher than the facade. Eventually, another architect was hired to see what he could do, which resulted in his placing a clock on each tower. The one on the right side of the basilica was called the Oltramontano clock, and the one on the left was known as the Italian clock.

It was 6:00 p.m. when Jacopo Greco, a twenty-seven-year-old mafia assassin of some repute, picked the lock on the elevator door leading to the Oltramontano clock tower and rolled his cleaning cart into the tight space. Dressed in a utilitarian maintenance uniform consisting of a dark blue shirt and pants and carrying a disassembled sniper rife within his cart supplies, he took the elevator to the observation platform. The bearded, thick-chested five feet ten assassin, who had Popeye arms and short black hair, carried photos of Bruno and Donati in his shirt pocket. These had been given to him by the *capodecina*, the head of his family branch within the mafia, with instructions that both men were to be killed as quickly as possible. The why wasn't important. To Greco, the only thing that mattered was that they ended up in the morgue.

From the information given to him, he knew that both targets were likely to be near St. Peter's Basilica or the Casa Santa Marta, although the exact time they would be there wasn't known. That didn't matter to him since he had more than enough provisions in the cart to stake out the two sites for days. After consulting an area map, Greco had selected the Oltramontano clock tower because it offered him the best opportunity to observe both areas where his targets were likely to be while remaining undetected. The fact that he had been able to get into the tower unobserved was a surprise because security was usually very diligent; this was why he had an ID badge for a nonexistent cleaning service clipped to his pocket. It was his favorite ruse, and if someone called the phone number on the badge to verify his employment, they'd be speaking to another mafia soldier. Today, however, since St. Peter's Square was closed to tourists, there was no security patrolling the area around the tower.

Five minutes after assembling his rifle and making a minor adjustment to the scope, he started scanning the square. That's when he saw Bruno and Donati, accompanied by another man to the right of them, walking from the basilica toward the Casa Santa Marta. He was sure it was them because both looked exactly like the photos he'd taken from his pocket. Resting his suppressed rifle on the ledge of the ornate balcony bordering the tower, he moved his finger onto the trigger. Judging from the Vatican flag drooping from its pole, there was no wind that would interfere with the bullet's trajectory. It was a textbook kill. He'd pop off two rounds and be gone before anyone knew what had happened. At least that was the plan. It disintegrated when the third man changed position so that he was now to the left of Bruno and Donati, thereby blocking Greco's view of the targets.

Greco didn't have a shot, and both targets eventually rounded the corner of a building and moved out of sight.

Although the mafia assassin was in his late twenties, he was a seasoned assassin by most standards, with over fifty kills to his credit. Therefore, as frustrated as he was that he hadn't gotten off a shot, Greco understood that his targets were walking dead now that he'd seen them. Taking a folded map of the Vatican from his back pocket, he saw that there was no other exit from the area to which they were headed. Therefore, they'd have to come back through the square. When they did, they'd be walking directly toward him.

As it turned out, Greco didn't have to live with his anxiety for long. Twenty minutes later, he spotted Bruno and Donati walking directly toward him, just as he had anticipated. They were targets on a shooting range. Greco stood, once again resting his gun on the chest-high balcony ledge, and started to slowly exhale as he gradually increased his pressure on the trigger. But Greco never got to completely exhale or put that last pound of pressure on the trigger because before he could complete either action, a large-caliber bullet shattered his nose and entered his brain. The assassin flew backward about four feet, slammed hard against the lower facade of the clock, and collapsed onto the floor of the balcony, lifeless.

Hunkler, Bruno, Donati, and the sniper who'd killed Greco were at the top of the Oltramontano clock tower, standing over Greco's corpse. Bruno and Donati's photos were lying on the floor not far from the body.

"It looks like the patriarch is holding a grudge against you two," Hunkler said, pointing to the photos.

"You haven't told us how you discovered that he was here," Bruno said to the sniper.

"Part of the job of our sniper team is to protect His Holiness not only from those who would attack him on the ground but also from other snipers. The pope left his residence not long after you visited him. Therefore, he was not far behind you, on his way to the basilica. Whenever he's going to be in the open, another sniper and I have designated positions that give us an unobstructed view of the crowd and surrounding structures. I'd just gotten into position when I saw someone in this tower with a rifle pointed into the square. No questions asked—I took the shot."

"Fortunately for the both of you, the pope was anxious to see what you reacquired for the church," Hunkler said. "He wanted to spend some time in the room by himself. I, of course, was accompanying him there when this incident occurred."

"This is just his first attempt at killing us," Bruno said. "I don't think the duke is going to stop until we're both dead. With his money and resources, it's only a matter of time before we end up in a pine box."

"What do you suggest?" Donati asked.

"That we change the rules of the game."

CHAPTER 22

THE PATRIARCH WAS sitting in his study, celebrating what he believed would soon be the deaths of Bruno and Donati with a spectacular Hennessy Beauté du Siécle Grand Champagne cognac, when his cell phone rang. He recognized the number as that of his mafia contact in Milan and expected to be told that Bruno and Donati had been killed. Instead, what he heard was that the assassin was the lone fatality. And just when he thought things couldn't get any worse, his contact said that he'd learned from one of his sources that an undisclosed number of written records on the duke had been turned over to the Polizia di Stato and that they would eventually be coming to his estate to arrest him. The patriarch ended the call without commenting, cutting his contact off midsentence.

After sitting in silence for several minutes, Rizzo poured himself another snifter of cognac and went to his desk. He removed two sheets of stationery, an envelope, postage, and his $8 million Tibaldi Fulgor Nocturnus fountain pen. The letter he composed showed no emotion and was factual in content. After he ran an ink blotter over what he'd written, he folded the pages, inserted them into the envelope, and affixed the proper postage. He then summoned one of the guards to drive him to the post office, which was ten minutes from the estate. He could have had the driver mail the envelope for him. But this letter was extremely sensitive, and he wanted to ensure that it got to the post office without being read. Therefore, he hand-delivered the letter to the postal clerk and immediately returned to the estate. There was one more thing there that he needed to do.

The Rome newspaper that broke the story wasn't especially large, but it did have a reputation for being accurate and unbiased, a rarity among its peers. Therefore, when it published pages from the patriarch's family dairies showing how the Rizzo family had historically embezzled from the church and killed anyone who could expose them—and then ended the story with the allegation that Duke Rodolfo Rizzo himself had been responsible for numerous murders to keep this family secret—it was like pouring blood into a pool of sharks. An army of press and paparazzi raced to the estate and surrounded it, in the belief that the patriarch's arrest would be imminent. Upon seeing the newspaper's exposé, the four guards who had composed the remainder of the duke's security detail had decided to leave before authorities could question them about their past activities. Therefore, by the time the paparazzi surrounded the house, Duke Rodolfo Rizzo was alone in his mansion.

The patriarch stood at the window of his office, looking out at the placid lake before him. He had known as soon as Bruno and Donati survived the attempt on their lives that they'd come after him. Rizzo had never believed for a moment that they had returned the diaries without at least copying some of the more explosive entries as an insurance policy, because that's what he would have done if their situations were reversed.

Legally, he had several options. He could sue the newspaper and claim that what they had been given was a forgery meant to discredit him and his family. His attorneys also could argue that these copies were inadmissible in court because they had been stolen and because the originals couldn't be produced to prove their authenticity. But in the arena of public opinion, none of this mattered. The duke's reputation was already shattered. His banking license was likely to be stripped away because the government didn't have to have an ironclad reason to do this. Again, he could fight that in court and technically win, but in the process he'd lose most of his personal and corporate customers. Their trust in him and his family's financial institution had, thanks to these accusations, already evaporated. Therefore, when they withdrew their assets, he'd sink below the minimum capital requirements, and the regulators would come in and administer the bank in his stead. The rest of his life would then be a series of endless legal proceedings.

Rizzo wasn't bothered by the armada of boats collecting on the lake, meaning that he was virtually surrounded and that there was no chance of escape. He had no intention of trying to get away. There was nowhere to hide. He was too infamous for that, and he wasn't going to live inside a spider hole for his entire life. Yesterday he'd already decided his next course of action, and today, for the family's survival, he was going to implement it.

He unhurriedly walked to the front door, unlocked it, then went back to his study. Most of his assets were hidden— they always were. With a few keystrokes on his computer, he had already functionally handed them over to his business partner, who was largely responsible for diversifying the family's holdings. He had then removed the computer's hard drive, smashed it, and taken a boat out onto the lake, where he threw the computer and smashed hard drive into the water. After that he'd had the altar and angels from the chapel removed and transported to his partner, along with the family diaries, works of art, and other treasures from the mansion. That task had been accomplished quickly and efficiently by several armored transport companies.

Reclining in his desk chair, the patriarch removed a gold-plated Beretta Px4 Storm Deluxe semiautomatic pistol from his desk drawer and placed it atop his desk. He picked it up without hesitation, gripped the handle firmly so that he'd have control of the weapon, held it under his chin, and pulled the trigger.

When a line of police cars left the Milan station and headed for the main highway, word quickly spread, and civilian vehicles started following behind them. The ten-car policy convoy therefore became a pied piper event led by Bruno and Donati; Donati was driving the lead vehicle, with Bruno sitting in the front passenger seat. The closer they got to the estate, the longer the caravan grew.

Bruno told Donati that he wasn't surprised at the response garnered by the newspaper article. Rizzo, for all his great wealth, was not a philanthropist and didn't have a kind bone in his body. Thus, no one liked the unempathetic and stingy billionaire. The inspectors' decision to put what they'd copied of the diaries into print had been about survival. With almost an unlimited amount of money, the duke could afford to keep sending assassins after them until one eventually succeeded. Therefore, they had decided to roll the dice and hope that the information they provided the newspaper would put Rizzo in the limelight and on the defensive, worried more about his financial survival than about killing them. But they agreed that if Rizzo could multitask, they wouldn't live out the year.

When they arrived at the estate, the local police had already cordoned it off and chased everyone off the piers, posting a patrol boat to keep everyone away. Fortunately, no one had yet entered the residence. Law enforcement stood in front of the gates to discourage anyone from attempting to climb them, although some managed to slip by. Those that did seemed more interested in exploring the estate than in entering the mansion. Donati, who had the Yukon XL's transponder in hand, opened the gates. He then drove up the long gravel driveway to the mansion, accompanied by four officers in two trailing vehicles. Arrest warrant in hand, they were there to take Rizzo into custody. The remaining officers in the caravan supplemented the local police, keeping people out of the estate and rounding up anyone they found beyond the gates and throwing them off the property.

Donati used the knocker to announce their presence. Not hearing a response, he tried turning the front door handle. He was prepared to break down the door but found that it was unlocked. All six entered, with Donati directing the officers to spread out and check the top floors of the mansion, while he went to Rizzo's office and Bruno went to his study.

When Bruno entered the study, he felt no surprise at finding the duke reclined in his desk chair, staring wide-eyed at the ceiling. There was very little blood, just a hole under his chin and no exit wound. The gun that had canceled his ticket to everyday life was lying on the floor beside him. Donati came in a few minutes later, just as Bruno, with Rizzo's wallet and security card in hand, was walking toward the RFID reader, having already pressed the button under the desk to retract the wall.

"It doesn't look like he was willing to go through the humiliation of a trial," Donati said, staring at Rizzo for a moment before joining Bruno at the vault.

"It doesn't surprise me. I half expected it. It was easier to die in these luxurious surroundings than in poverty or in a dank prison cell," Bruno replied, holding the RFID card in front of the reader and watching the vault door open.

When they looked inside, they found only empty shelves.

"I have a sinking feeling," Bruno said as he left the study and headed for the chapel, followed by Donati.

Opening the chapel's large bronze doors, they found that both the altar and the angels were missing.

"Did you see any artwork on the corridor walls?" Donati asked.

"Come to think of it, no."

"Since he obviously couldn't take it with him, someone has just been handed a fortune."

"Hopefully, we aren't on their radar," Bruno said.

"If we are, we'll never see it coming. Not with that much money behind someone bent on revenge."

On that they agreed.

The person who received the handwritten letter from Duke Rodolfo Rizzo hadn't been expecting it, but neither was he surprised, given the story in the newspaper and his last conversation with the now deceased duke. He generally knew what the letter would say and opened it with a steady hand. He read both pages with no outward expression of emotion and then folded the letter and returned it to its envelope. The task that had been given to him would not be easy to accomplish and would take a great deal of money. Fortunately, that wasn't an issue. He already had been quite wealthy even before armored transports delivered the contents of the chapel, the family diaries, the works of art, and various other valuables from the Rizzo estate earlier today. All that, along with the businesses, precious metals, antiques, stocks, bearer bonds, and extensive foreign bank accounts currently under his control, meant that he was one of the wealthiest of the world's multibillionaires. He didn't believe that anger solved anything, but he did believe in revenge.

Indro Montanari was free—released from the Regina Coeli prison three years ahead of schedule and without parole, just as Bruno had promised. The chief inspector was there as Montanari walked out the freedom gate, as the prisoners called it, and the two walked to a small café several blocks away, where Bruno ordered two cups of espresso.

"Thank you for keeping your word," Montanari said after the waiter left their table, "and for picking me up."

"It seemed the least I could do. Salud!" Bruno said, touching his cup to Montanari's.

Each took a sip of their espresso.

"Have you given any thought to what you're going to do?" asked Bruno.

"I haven't. I didn't believe that I'd be released early, despite what you told me. When the guard came to my cell a few hours ago and gave me the news, I thought he was playing a joke on me. Then when I found out that he wasn't, my mind went in a hundred different directions. I'm still trying to catch up with reality."

"Understandable. You're extremely talented, and there are many companies—and government agencies for that matter—that need protection from people such as the person you once were. With that in mind, you might want to call this person." Bruno handed Montanari a business card that Colonel Andrin Hunkler had earlier given him. "I spoke with the colonel this morning. The Vatican's security system is apparently very antiquated, and he could use a good consultant to help him design and implement a new one. If you want to be an employee instead, I believe he'd also be amenable to that. Either way, you have a job."

Unable to control his emotions, Montanari took off his glasses and wiped the moisture from his eyes with a napkin. "Grazie" was all he could say in response as he started to sob.

Donati pulled to the curb at the Milan train station and turned off the engine. The black BMW 528i coupe that he was driving was a duplicate of his earlier car, minus the dents and bullet holes that had sent its predecessor to the scrap yard.

"Your train for Venice departs in thirty minutes from track one. Before you leave, I wanted to thank you for what you did," Donati said, unfastening his seat belt and turning slightly to his right to face Bruno. "Without your help, I doubt I would have been able to solve these murders and prove the patriarch's involvement, even though you've publicly given me credit for doing just that."

"You saved my life and helped to find who was responsible for my father's death—that more than balances the scales," Bruno said. "In the past several days I've heard your colleagues refer to you as a good officer, Elia. But to live the hard and dangerous life that comes with being a police officer, when you could have chosen a life of luxury, makes you an extraordinary officer in my book. I'd be honored to work with you again. If you ever need my help, I'm a phone call away."

"A gracious offer, although my father's insurance company might not be excited about you returning to Milan," he said, patting the steering wheel of his car. "Your father's neighbors also might have an issue—something about a gunfight on their street. I also seem to recall a complaint I received from a funeral home director about a shooting outside his business. And let's not forget the cemetery."

"I get it," Bruno said. "I'll stay in Venice."

"Not at all. My life is far too stagnant without you around."

Bruno opened the door and got out of the BMW with his carry-on bag and his father's Floto Firenze briefcase. He then took an envelope out of his pocket and handed it to Donati.

"What is it?" Donati said, taking the envelope.

Bruno ignored the question, giving Donati a final wave goodbye before heading toward his train.

When Bruno was out of sight, Donati opened the letter. Inside was a copy of an email Bruno had received from Rome, indicating that his recommendation that Inspector Elia Donati be promoted to chief inspector had been granted and was effective immediately.

CHAPTER 23

SIX MONTHS AND two weeks after Bruno and Donati last saw each other, they met at the Ritz Paris for a one-week celebration of both Donati's promotion and Bruno's birthday. Donati was no stranger to the Ritz, since he and his family went there yearly between Christmas and New Year. Their adjoining rooms on the first floor provided convenient access to the lavish hotel's bars, restaurants, and spa.

Bruno was the last to check in, and after he got settled, he and Donati decided to go to the spa and get a massage to begin their week of relaxation. Both were dressed in swimming trunks, a hotel robe, and slippers as they walked down the hall outside their rooms. They were nearly to the elevator when they heard a scream coming from the last room on the right. The door was open, and a maid's cart was to the side of the doorway. Rushing into the room, they saw the housekeeper standing over the prone body of a man whose open eyes were fixated on the bed across from him. The deceased was well dressed, wearing an elegant blue suit and open-collared light blue shirt. A small amount of blood was visible on the floor and apparently had flowed from under the body.

Bruno bent down and checked for a pulse but found none. Judging from the coldness of the body and the pallor of the man's skin, Bruno and Donati agreed that the man had been dead for several hours. Neither chief inspector wanted to move him or try to determine the cause of death. This wasn't their case. They'd leave those tasks to the French police.

The housekeeper, who had seemed borderline hysterical, had run past them and out of the room soon after Bruno bent down to check for the nonexistent pulse. Neither inspector knew whether she'd already summoned help or was just now going to get it. Judging from the speed at which she had left, both thought it was the latter.

"This hotel is a gathering place for people of importance— actors, billionaires, chairmen, and CEOs of multinational corporations. Anyone who comes to Paris and matters stays here," Donati said. "So it's inconceivable that the hotel wouldn't have an extensive camera system. I'm betting every hallway in this building is surveilled. If the killer had any smarts at all, they'd know or suspect that."

"A crime of passion. A business or marital dispute. That'd be my focus," Bruno responded. "But since it's my birthday, and my friend is so generously picking up the tab for my stay, I'm happy to let the Paris police make their own deductions without my input. Now, I believe our masseuses are waiting."

"They might have to wait a while longer," Donati said, taking two photos off the desk to the right of the victim and showing them to Bruno.

Bruno looked at the high-resolution hand-sized photos with incredulity. "Why would he have our pictures?"

"A good question. Nevertheless, if they see these, the police will believe that we know more than we do," Donati said as he put the photos in the pocket of his robe. "They may even believe this implicates us in the murder."

"How did this person know we were here?"

Donati shrugged his shoulders.

They decided to quickly search the room to see what else they might find before the housekeeper returned with help. The victim apparently had traveled light because the only luggage they found was an old black ballistic nylon shoulder bag. Donati opened the bag. Inside were a few personal items along with a dozen sheets of paper. Donati removed the papers from the bag, and his eyes opened wide when he saw that they were foreign bank statements showing that he and Bruno each had one million US dollars sitting in offshore accounts. "We're rich," Donati said, handing the pages to Bruno.

"Does this remind you of anything?" Bruno asked.

Donati nodded, the look on his face confirming that he shared Bruno's suspicions.

Hearing fast footsteps coming up the stairs adjacent to the room, Bruno quickly folded the pages and put them in his robe pocket.

The housekeeper was followed into the room by an elegantly dressed man who identified himself as the manager of the hotel and two police officers, who requested that Bruno and Donati remain in the room until the detectives arrived. Accustomed to police procedures, both chief inspectors sat on the edge of the bed and waited. Five minutes later, two medical personnel arrived and, after verifying that the man with the open eyes and pool of blood under him was indeed dead, left. No sooner were they out the door than the medical examiner arrived, accompanied by two detectives and a forensic technician.

Bruno and Donati identified themselves as chief inspectors with Italy's Polizia di Stato. Judging from the look of indifference on the detectives' faces, that didn't carry any weight. The detectives separated Donati and Bruno, paired off with them, and questioned the two on opposite sides of the room.

The questioning stopped when the medical examiner turned the body over, exposing a large pool of blood and the apparent cause of death—a gunshot wound to the heart. In the center of the pool of blood was a handgun. The photographer, who was taking photos during this time, moved his lens close to the weapon and took a series of photos before indicating that he had what he needed. Next up was the forensic technician, who removed a plastic evidence bag and, with a gloved hand, placed the gun into it.

Ignoring Bruno and Donati for the moment, the detectives both looked at the evidence bag and saw that it contained a suppressed Beretta 92FS with the initials "E. D." engraved on the right grip. The initials were large, so Bruno and Donati were able to see them from where they were standing. But unlike their Paris counterparts, they knew exactly to whom the weapon belonged: Elia Donati.

After ten minutes of questioning, Bruno and Donati were told they could go after writing down their room and cell phone numbers on a piece of paper handed to them. They were also instructed not to leave Paris.

They went to Bruno's room and sat on the edge of his bed.

"How did your gun get here?" Bruno asked Donati.

"It was stolen in a break-in at my home a month ago. I have no idea where the suppressor came from. Whoever did this is good. You can bet that my fingerprints will be on the weapon."

"Couple the murder weapon with the photos and the bank statements, and it's the perfect frame. It would be better if they didn't find the photos or the bank papers."

Donati said he agreed and took the photos from the pocket of his robe and handed them to Bruno. Finding a plastic bag in the closet, Bruno placed the statements and photos inside. He then opened the door to the balcony, where a flowerbox stretched from one end to the other, pulled up one of the artificial begonias, and placed the bag underneath it.

An hour later, as if on cue, there was a knock on the door. When Bruno opened it, he saw the detective who had taken Donati's statement, along with two police officers.

"Chief Inspector Elia Donati," said the detective in a formal tone as he looked past Bruno to the person sitting on the edge of the bed. "You're under arrest for murder."

Donati was silent.

One of the officers cuffed Donati. With an officer holding each of his arms, and still in his robe and slippers, Donati was perp-walked out of the hotel and into a waiting police car.

AUTHOR'S NOTE

This is a work of fiction, and the people and companies mentioned within are not meant to depict any person, organization, or circumstance in the real world.

Ever since Chief Inspector Mauro Bruno was introduced in *The Archivist*, the author has received numerous pleas that Bruno be given his own series of novels. Readers found him far too interesting a character to be relegated to a single book. The author was happy to comply and hopes that you have found this novel as fun to read as it was to write. The idea for the ending came about after a stay at the Ritz Paris, where the author got the sense that the storied hotel would be an intriguing place for a murder mystery. *The Scion*, the next book in the Mauro Bruno detective series, picks up where *The Patriarch* leaves off.

The author first got the inspiration for *The Patriarch's* storyline while taking a private tour of the Vatican. As the guide delved into early Catholicism, she mentioned Saint Helena and the True Cross, along with some of the more nefarious aspects of papal history. How could the author resist combining both?

If you haven't been to Milan, you should put it on your bucket list. Beyond the magnificence of the Duomo, a Gothic-style cathedral that took almost six hundred years to complete, Da Vinci's *Last Supper* is stunning and is alone worth the trip. The Park Hyatt is, as indicated, near both city hall and La Scala Opera. It is also adjacent to the Galleria Vittorio Emanuele II, the world's oldest active shopping mall, a four-story double arcade built between 1865 and 1877. If you like shopping for designer goods, the first Prada store, Fratelli Prada, opened in this mall in 1913 and is still there, along with much of the original cabinetry.

Even though Acquolina is fictitious, Milan has many spectacular restaurants whose cuisine and service are world-class. The author's favorites include Cracco, Il Luogo di Aimo e Nadi, and Langosteria.

Mezzegra is a lovely town in the Lake Como area, approximately forty miles from Milan. But Saint Benedict's does not exist. Its description is a compilation of several monasteries in Italy that the author visited. The narrow mountain road connecting Mezzegra to Milan is also fictional.

The restaurant La Veranda and its terrace at the Four Seasons Milan are as described. The hotel is within walking distance of the Duomo, one of the most magnificent cathedrals in the world.

Hennessy Beauté du Siécle Grand Champagne cognac is real and is extraordinarily rare and expensive. Each bottle is made of Baccarat crystal and is accompanied by a set of four glasses, each adorned with gold leaf and aluminum. The rare liquid and glasses are housed in a spectacular chest of melted aluminum and glass, topped by two colored Venetian glass beads. The youngest bottle of this cognac is forty-seven years old, and the oldest one hundred years. Its average retail price is $111,046. That price climbs significantly with older bottles, however.

Bellagio sits on the landmass that divides Lake Como. It is beautiful and extraordinarily romantic. There is no mansion such as the author described, nor is there an exit off the highway that leads to a twisting two-lane road. Both were concocted by the author for the sake of the storyline. Duke Rodolfo Rizzo's estate was modeled, in part, after the Villa d'Este Hotel on Lake Como, which sits in a twenty-five-acre private park. It doesn't get any better than sitting on the hotel's terrace watching the sun set and then retreating to the veranda restaurant for dinner.

Helena Augusta, also referred to as St. Helena, was the mother of Emperor Constantine, who seized power in AD 312 and legalized Christianity with the Edict of Milan. According to Eusebius, a church historian, while in Palestine in AD 326 Helena demolished the Temple of Venus, which was built upon Mount Calvary. Just east of this site, she discovered three crosses in a rock cistern, along with a wooden plaque with the inscription "Jesus Nazaranus Rex Iudaeorum." Therefore, in the minds of many, she'd found the True Cross. As to the question of which cross held the corporeal body of Christ, St. John Chrysostom provides the story that the three crosses and the titulus were removed from the cistern, and a dying woman touched each of them. She was reportedly cured after putting her hand on the third cross, thereby identifying it as the one on which Jesus died. St. Helena, again according to the historian Eusebius, returned to Rome, where she built the Basilica of the Holy Cross in Jerusalem, located a few blocks from the Basilica of Saint John Lateran, and placed inside what she fervently believed to be the True Cross. She also displayed there what she and others believed to be two thorns from the crown placed on Christ's head, a nail used in the crucifixion, a remnant of the cross of the repentant thief, stone fragments of the scourging pillar, and the Titulus Crucis, the wooden inscription written in Hebrew, Greek, and Latin.

The description of Clement XII's age and health is accurate. He went blind seven years prior to his death and did suffer from gout, finally dying from complications relating to this illness and not from being poisoned. It is widely believed that he was elected pope at the advanced age of seventy-eight because the conclave couldn't agree on anyone else who would be acceptable to two-thirds of those voting for pope, the percentage necessary to elect a pontiff. Many believe that Lorenzo Corsini was selected because he was not expected to live long, and his anticipated short reign would give the cardinals enough time to agree on a successor. But Clement XII surprised them and held the throne for ten years. He is buried in the Basilica of St. John Lateran in Rome. His secretary of state was not Cardinal Casaroli, who is a fictional character. There is no evidence that the secretaries of state for Pope Benedict XIII or Pope Clement XII did anything illicit. But when Cardinal Lorenzo Corsini became the bishop of Rome, the church's finances were indeed in ruins. The chief culprit in depleting the treasury was Cardinal Niccolò Coscia, whom Pope Clement heavily fined and sentenced to ten years in prison. The pontiff then reinstituted the public lottery as a way of raising money, and soon the church was awash in half a million scudi, the currency of the Papal States until 1866, when it was replaced by the Italian lira.

The process described for the certification of the death of a pope is accurate.

The Porta Romana area of Milan is a historic district adjacent to the city center, which does have nineteenth- and early-twentieth-century buildings. These are used as offices or residences by the well-heeled Milanese elite. There are no pocket residential neighborhoods, each composed of a dozen or so individual homes, within this district.

When Italy became independent in 1861, Milan decided to consolidate its numerous smaller cemeteries into two—the Cimitero Monumentale for the wealthy and the Cimitero Maggiore for commoners. As you might imagine, the wealthy families tried to artistically outdo each other by hiring some of the world's most famous artists to design and build their sculptures, tombs, and mausoleums. This created what amounted to an immense open-air museum that is well worth seeing. Some liberty was taken in describing the chapel at the Cimitero Monumentale, as well as its location in relation to the Catholic portion of the cemetery, for the sake of the storyline.

The Archivum Secretum Apostolicum Vaticanum, or Vatican Secret Archives as it is generally called, exists and is enormous, necessitating fifty-three miles of shelving to house its volumes. But the name is somewhat misleading. When the Latin is translated to English, *secretum* becomes *private*. Therefore, Vatican Private Archives is probably a more accurate translation. This makes sense since it is owned by the pope until he dies or resigns, and it is for his private use. Its location is as depicted. The Vatican's original reference number for the Chinon Parchment, which is accurately described, is Archivum Arcis Armarium D 217. As noted, it was discovered by Barbara Frale, an Italian paleographer at the Vatican Secret Archives, after it was misfiled. The author couldn't resist using the same location for what Cardinal Casaroli hid.

The Order of Saint Benedict is as described, in that it's not a single religious organization because each monastery operates autonomously. The abbot primate, the senior monk, is elected by all to that office and acts as a liaison to the Vatican.

The Vatican has two security forces—the Gendarmerie and the Swiss Guards. The Gendarmerie is a police and security force. Within Vatican City, its officers ensure order at meetings, ceremonies, and other gatherings to protect those in attendance. In addition, when the pope travels, they coordinate with local police forces. In contrast, the Swiss Guard's primary responsibility is the safety of the pope as well as the Apostolic Palace. All members are required to be Catholic and unmarried Swiss citizens who have completed Swiss military service. They also must be at least five feet, eight inches tall and be between nineteen and thirty years of age. In this book the author at times combined functions of the Gendarmerie and Swiss Guards to simplify the storyline.

As written, the current pope lives in suite 201 at the Casa Santa Marta. The two-room suite within the hotel-style residence next to St. Peter's Basilica is in stark contrast to the Vatican's Apostolic Palace used by previous popes—a spectacular penthouse apartment complex with more than a dozen rooms and a sweeping view of Rome.

Half the residences in the Casa Santa Marta are occupied by Vatican staff, while the rest are used by visiting clergy and laypeople. The pope tends to eat many of his meals, from what we know, in the communal dining room. The author has taken some liberties with the internal description of the two-room residence. The description was orchestrated from publicly available information and photographs, then extrapolated for the sake of the storyline.

The pope does have a sign outside his door at the Vatican indicating that complaining is forbidden and that "violators are subject to a syndrome of always feeling like a victim." The remainder of the text is as indicated, noting that offenders "are subject to developing a victim complex, resulting in a lowering ... of their capacity to solve problems ... the penalty is doubled whenever the violation is committed in the presence of children." It goes on to explain, "To be your best you have to focus on your own potential and not on your limits, so stop whining and act to make your life better."

The Vatican Grottoes, the Vatican Necropolis, and Field P are as described. But there is no door adjacent to the site said to contain the bones of Saint Peter and therefore no key that has been passed down from pontiff to pontiff. Those details were created for the sake of the storyline.

As indicated, Bernini designed two monumental towers, one to stand on either side of St. Peter's Basilica. But because the ground could not bear the weight of these structures, they never rose above the line of the facade. Later, Giuseppe Valadier designed two clocks, one to sit on either side of the front facade. The clock on the right is known as the Oltramontano clock, while the one on the left is called the Italian clock.

The Ritz Paris is spectacular, and readers will experience more of this hotel in the next Mauro Bruno and Elia Donati novel. The hotel staff is extremely personable and friendly and can point you to sites and experiences that would be difficult to encounter on your own. If I had to pick one hotel in the world in which to reside, this would be it. But the Bauer Il Palazzo in Venice is within a hair's width.

ACKNOWLEDGEMENTS

An author doesn't work in a vacuum. In my case, I've been blessed with amazing friends who continue to be, book after book, my sounding board. "Thank you" doesn't begin to cover my appreciation for their comments.

To Kerry Refkin, my loving wife: I'm extraordinarily grateful to you for your expert edits and fine-tuning of the storyline. You *are* amazing.

To the group: Thank you again for your valuable insights— Scott Cray, Dr. Charles and Aprille Pappas, Dr. John and Cindy Cancelliere, Doug Ballinger, Alexandra Parra, Mark Iwinski, Mike Calbot, Dr. Meir Daller, Ed Houck, and Cheryl Rinell.

To Zhang Jingjie for her research: Thank you for continuing to ferret out facts that give substance to my descriptions.

To Dr. Kevin Hunter and Rob Durst, I'm grateful for your computer, cybersecurity, and IT support. Thank you again for explaining what I would consider the unexplainable.

To Clay Parker, Jim Bonaquist, Steve Zhu, and Greg Urbancic: Thank you for the extraordinary legal advice you provide.

To Bill Wiltshire and Debbie Layport: Thanks again for your superb financial and accounting skills.

To our friends Zoran Avramoski, Piotr Cretu, Aleksandar Toporovski, Neti Gaxholli, and Billy DeArmond: Thanks for your insights.

To Winnie and Doug Ballinger and Scott and Betty Cray: Continued thanks for all you do for the countless people who are unable to fend for themselves. The hundreds of people that you've helped will have a better life because of what you've done. Bravo!

ABOUT THE AUTHOR

Alan Refkin is the author of five previous works of fiction and the coauthor of four business books on China. He received an Editor's Choice Award for *The Wild Wild East* and for *Piercing the Great Wall of Corporate China*. The author and his wife, Kerry, live in southwest Florida. More information on the author, including his blogs, can be found at alanrefkin.com.

Printed in the United States
By Bookmasters